Also by Eileen Saint Lauren

Fiction   *Goodlife, Mississippi A Novel*

Southern, Light, Oxford, Mississippi A Novel

MY NEIGHBORS, GOODLIFE, MISSISSIPPI

Stories

MY NEIGHBORS,
GOODLIFE, MISSISSIPPI

Stories

Eileen Saint Lauren

EILEEN SAINT LAUREN BOOKS
CHAPEL HILL, NC (USA)

EILEEN SAINT LAUREN BOOKS
CHAPEL HILL, NC (USA)

MY NEIGHBORS, GOODLIFE, MISSISSIPPI Stories
Copyright © 2023 Eileen Saint Lauren

ISBN 979-8-9861963-3-6
1. Southern Gothic — Fiction, Stories. 2. Literature of the American South — African American, Segregation, Mississippi. 3. Magical Realism. I. Title.

Book Design by Arash Jahani

Unless otherwise noted, the Bible version used in this publication is THE KING JAMES VERSION, Copyright © 1972 Thomas Nelson, Inc., Publishers.

*Dedicated to the memory of the folks I grew up
visiting with Momma in South Mississippi whose
stories I have never forgotten.*

CONTENTS

Thou shalt love thy neighbour as thyself.
—*Matthew* 22:39.

MY NEIGHBORS, GOODLIFE, MISSISSIPPI

Stories

PROLOGUE

Dear Reader,

In Goodlife, Mississippi, sits a world without end. It is where I live and write. Goodlife is 1500 miles square, with a center that has yet to be entered.

I am surrounded by the throwaways, the downtrodden, and the lonely souls—some dead, some alive. I love them, and they love me. From day one, all the voices—the Black and the White—struck me as blue roses, all seemingly stuck somewhere in time. After all my folks died in Meridian, Mississippi, I moved to Goodlife to live with my elderly grandfolks where I came to believe that my purpose was to listen, and my calling was to write.

Early on, I wanted to be connected to someone, something, somebody by the way of love, the kind which is brotherly and unconditional. But all I saw growing up in one notch of the Bible Belt was twisted and conditional love, that is, until I began my own journey learning the secret things of God amid my neighbors.

People ask me, "What do you write about? What do you have to say?"

I write about Love—a love so deep and so pure that most people never experience it at all. What I have to say is that all that matters in any world is being loved. Love is what every soul dead or alive—desires— unconditional love.

My name is Mary Myra Boone, but you can call me Myra. I hope that you will read on and meet my neighbors.

Myra Boone
Goodlife, Mississippi 39480

MOZELLA

Peace

"**Y**ou *at peace*—Myra Boone?" Mozella asked me amid the lavender.

I frowned.

"If you wuz, you'd know it," she went on, gathering the pale blue, purple flowers.

"I suppose," was all I said.

The early light began to reflect off her old blue-black face, making it look like a Roman soldier—hard and ready for battle. She was wearing a saffron-yellow apron over a date-brown shift dress. A dusty blue bonnet with a single red rose topped her silver head of hair. She carried a hump of sorts in the middle of her back as if it were a newborn baby. And a bronzed colored scarf was tied in three rings around her neck like a trinity wedding band.

"How long you been gathering the lavender in for the Reynolds' Mercantile?" I asked her.

"Ever since Moeris sang his last song."

"Oh."

I had heard that her old man had died long ago, and I didn't want to cause her any *remembering* pain if I could help it, so I kept silent.

"Ain't you going to ask me when that was?" she asked me.

"I wasn't planning on it," I told her.

She beamed.

I smiled, watching her little pinched blue-black face take on more of the early light like a Monet painting, but still, I didn't speak. Instead, I shrugged my shoulders and brushed the lavender with my right hand, feeling some of the morning's dew lick my fingertips.

"I been getting' up pretty near 4:30 every morning for thirty year or more to get in the lavender when it be the season. You know what I think about here lately?"

"No."

"I think about my Poppadaddy back in 1875 when he worked in a cantaloupe field in due season. Then he brung in the cotton in Laurel, Mississippi, at one of Buster Farmer's Plantations with summers as hot as hell fire."

"Oh."

"Poppadaddy was good to me and Momma—he especially like to build things—you know what I mean?"

I nodded.

"When I was a young girl—slim *and* trim—" Mozella grinned, patting her big behind then dropping some lavender.

I laughed out loud.

When she reached for the flowers a whiff of purple sweetness ran beneath my nose.

"I used to dream and dream and dream looking into my doll house. Oh, Myra, it was so fine! Momma and me made our own little furniture with bark from a quince tree. And sometimes, we used olive wood if we could find a smooth branch. We painted the house yellow to match the sun's glow and the furniture all sorts of bright, glowing colors we made from the flowers and such."

I nodded.

"Poppadaddy called me his *Wonder-Chile*," she told me then added, "Because I measured *big* by little things." She tapped her breast once.

"Really?"

She chaffed her lips on a blade of tender green grass.

"I did. And he would come in on a Friday night with a pocket full of change tinkling like crystal and pennies then say to me, 'Mozella, if you guess how much money I got in my britches pocket, it's yours!'"

"One red-cent," I'd guess.

"A penny?"

She laughed. "I was never right. And rightly so—I wouldn't have taken his money for the world, so I never even tried to guess right!"

"You funny!"

"You thank?"

"I do."

She beamed. "Would you like some soup?"

"For breakfast?"

"Why not?"

"Well, I don't know..."

I looked up and a marigold sun was just before spinning against a sad Mississippi azure blue sky. The green pines were not going to offer us enough shadows to shade us from the flaming heat that followed every early light. So, I said, "Sure, Mozella, some soup would be nice."

"I have some with me—in a snuff jar."

I frowned, surprised.

Holding up a little jar she'd had in her pocket that contained a cloudy liquid of sorts, she told me, "Let's go to the graveyard and visit Moeris. We can share the goods."

"All right then."

"Oh, good! I brewed up some pounded garlic and just a smidgen of wild-thyme with lamb broth. And I got a pone of oven-baked cornbread—we can share, hear?"

"That sounds real nice. Yes, real nice, Mozella," I told her.

"It should be right pretty in the cemetery right about now— peaceful."

"I suppose."

"Let's go," she told me, tying up her lavender. She walked over and hid it in the Piney Woods of Goodlife.

"Is it safe there?" I asked her.

"Why Myra Boone, you can't ask for nary thang better in this old world than the Piney Woods—don't you know?"

I shrugged.

We walked on for about three miles until we came to the oldest graveyard, I'd ever laid my eyes on. Entering through its gates of sleep, I saw that some of the headstones had pale garnets imbedded in them with free-roaming ivy gracing the strangest names I'd ever seen like *Purple Thankful, Ebenezer Dickinson, Roxanna Davis, Maces Dove, Emeline* and *Abigail*, and *Lucy*.

I looked over at Mozella, and she was heading for the middle of the graveyard. She stopped directly under an elm, looking up to see a turtledove cooing in its branches.

"My happy one!" she yelled, scaring the dove away.

An early morning breeze began to sing, gently. I felt my heart jump but not yet wearied by the beginning of a promising, scorching hot day *and* our long walk. I saw one grave that had a basketful of lilies and pale irises on it, and strangely enough, there was a plum tree growing in the center of another grave. And there was a weighed-down bush of blue roses beside an old oak tree.

"My heart is heavy-laden—here," she told me then added, "*With madness.*"

Mozella won't hurt me, will she?

"Madness?"

"Moeris treated me with such contempt—and the love he give to me still burns me slam up!"

"Mercy!"

"It do. I was as modest as anybody could be—I swear I was," she began.

"Let's eat the soup," I suggested.

"Like blue and yellow—I was hungry for the rain—but it never came as long as I was with him," she said soft and low before adding, "I chose to be hard of hearing..." Then she stopped talking, reached into her front pocket and brought back the snuff jar, and unscrewed its lid, but not before walking over to a small grave and plopping down on it.

I watched her close.

"I learn't to praise the man—I learn't it because he used to say to me, 'Mozella, all I want is peace—peace. Can't you give me peace?' I tried and I tried, but for the strength of me, I could not! Like a trader will forsake his sea, one cold spring Monday morning I up and left the man who held my heart, heading straight for Goodlife simply because I'd heard I could get me a job gathering in the lavender and such along the Way. Mind you, I didn't even take my best goat with me."

I motioned for the snuff jar.

She gave it to me.

I drank.

She turned and looked into the headstone which was carved in the shape of a diamond. Her body took on the shape of a willow tree, and a south wind joined us, strong and fast, causing her saffron apron to stir and whisper against her legs.

"He was so like an unknown god to me, yet powerful like a wild boar."

She took the last swallow of soup.

I listened.

"One day, Moeris began to conjure up spirits from deep down *within* the earth, his peace left him, and he blamed me."

I felt very thirsty from the soup but didn't mention it.

She sighed.

Without thinking, I asked, "Mozella, don't you have anyone to love you?"

Her eyes widened and welled up with silver tears before she said, "God loves me and that's enough."

"Really?"

She considered then said, "Who do you thank give me the courage to go on? To hold my head up after he come to Goodlife to take me back with him to New Orleans?"

I wiped my mouth with the tips of my fingers, and a whiff of lavender took my breath.

Reaching into her pocket and bringing out a pone of corn bread with tears streaming down her cheeks, she cried out, "Only God!"

"Oh."

She reached, and one by one untied the three rings of the bronze scarf. She slowly turned towards me, lifting her neck as if to offer me a smile and I saw the most awful scar across her throat. It was thick, silvered purple yet a pinkish-white and showy.

"Mozella, what in the world happened to your neck?!"

Putting the pone back into her pocket, she told me, "Like I said, Moeris come to Goodlife to carry me back to New Orleans... I wouldn't give in and go—I was strong. But like a trusting fool, I let him spend the night with me. The moon was full, gold, and glorious against a black powerful sky. I heard him get up—to get the can to pee—so I thought. Then, when he came back to me, he got on top of this one Negro woman and commenced to beg me to go back with him... I screamed out, and as best as I can guess, he'd brung a razor blade from the dresser bureau that I used to cut the thread when I hemmed my dresses and such."

I closed my eyes. And when I opened them, I could see that her neck still was holding a vicious scar that ran from ear to ear.

I gasped.

"Moeris told me, '*Mozella—I had you first—you shan't betray me for no one!*' Then he slit my throat." She lightly traced the silvered scar, setting her eyes straight on a headstone that read *Emeline and Abigail, Born April 4, 1900,* before saying, "These are my girls—I delivered them myself one bright winter's night, but no one ever knowed—till you. Still, I love my baby girls with their tiny silver dollar faces... That's why we here."

I didn't speak.

"When I come to, one of Ed Reynolds's *doctoring* friends had done gone and sewed up my throat. I believe he said it took one-hundredth and eighty-three stitches—," she told me.

I looked away at a maroon crepe myrtle tree that was in full bloom.

"...what *ought* I to have done, then?" Mozella asked me.

"*Prayed?*" I replied.

"Myra Boone—you don't, nor will you ever know jud'st how many times I prayed but Moeris' feet were firm. I wasn't able to stand my ground because he had the entire neighborhood of spiritual darkness on his side—voodoo magicians, beautiful nymphs, no shepherds or trusting lads, only water sprites, and other evil spirits..."

"Oh."

"I ain't denying that I may or may not have done (what he thought) *betrayed* him meant for beings my mind got silly girlish notions and fancy pictures in it from time to time..."

I stood up.

"Like the Bible says—Whatsoever a man thinketh in his heart so is he'—*and* you know how my neighbor, Ed Reynolds, be partial to Negro women like me with crisp dollar bills."

I frowned and walked over to trace the headstone with the pale garnets in it when I spotted a fluffy, (almost warm) gray squirrel. The squirrel scurried towards me in a starved way which made me feel like I was about to fall short because of my lack. Out of habit, I thrust my hands into my pockets, but they came back empty. Mozella searched hers and pulled out the pone of cornbread we'd forgotten to eat.

"Here," she offered me.

The squirrel didn't move a hair. I took the bread and broke off a quarter of it before she reached into her back pocket and brought out a little cowhide Bible.

Waving the Bible at me, she said, "A hand."

I took it and put a quarter of the cornbread on top of the Bible and offered it to the gray squirrel.

Mozella smiled to herself and reached for her bronze scarf.

The squirrel may have been as hungry as Cooter Brown, but he backed away from the Good Book—spooked.

"Put it down on the Earth and let him take it for himself."

"All right then," I said and did as I was told.

We waited.

The turtledove flew over our heads and settled in the plum tree and cooed soft and low. The squirrel boldly walked over and took his taste of bread. Then, it ran back across the graveyard, sat up on its haunches in front of an old oak tree and proceeded to enjoy his find in Nature's way—in solitude—right next to the blue roses.

Mozella said, "You still ain't said one word 'bout my neck—Myra Boone."

"What to say?"

"Do I look scary or naked or what without my scarf?"

I thought a moment then said, "No, Mozella—you don't scare me none..."

She smiled; lips rosy yet moist from the soup that had stayed with them. She got excited and interrupted me with, "How do I look, then?"

I stared into her face and could plainly see how enduring a soul she was. Bells began to fill the air—seven in all—like a clear warning for me to keep my mouth shut. I looked down at my feet before my eyes settled back onto my ugly, scarred hands.

Eyeing a nearby church house, she asked me, "Well?"

I lifted my head and looked around the graveyard and saw all shapes and sizes of trees that made lonely silhouettes like silent but seeing people against the blue-domed Goodlife azure blue sky that was still holding tight to the marigold sun that had finally begun to spin and spray us with the morning's new golden light.

Again, she asked, "Well?"

I took a long look into her face which, strangely enough, reminded me of a timber wolf.

She pierced her top lip with her eye teeth.

"At peace, Mozella—you look at peace."

She grinned like a goddess, reached into the bosom of her dress, and brought out a little wood carving of a water pitcher that was painted silver. She eyed it with loving eyes, close and trusting and sure. She kissed it and then said, "For you — from me and Poppadaddy."

I shook my head no.

She said, "Go on — take it."

"No."

"You must — Poppadaddy always told me that if I ever should find a listening friend that I was to pass it along. Myra Boone — you be my first real friend in Goodlife."

So, I took the little silver water pitcher that was clearly carved from an olive branch and held it up in the air against the big, blue-domed sky and turned it playfully against all the lonely trees. And, while I admired it, it began to twinkle like a star of grace amid the secrets of the air.

Mozella reached and took the red rose from her dusty blue bonnet and blissfully took a whiff. Then, she twirled it over and over until it broke in half hanging upside down like Nero's words.

I reached down and picked up her Bible, shook the breadcrumbs from its cover, and handed it back to her.

And we headed on back to Goodlife walking on the rays of a beautiful sun to gather in the lavender from its safe place in the woods.

CYRUS BLOOD

Provision

With the face of a blue rose and eyes glowing like the moon, Cyrus Blood, *gently* told Johnny Paul Russell and me this.

"Myra Boone, I weren't but six year old when the world opened to me and my Ma, Sophia, disappeared, leaving me alone on an azure day in the Piney Woods with only the voices and eyes of the animals to raise me in the Field of Lush where miracles thrive amid the secrets of the air."

I nodded, carefully arranging the ten apples we'd brought over to him in a pretty green Depression glass bowl.

Johnny Paul Russell sat as still as a church mouse on the floor. I sat down beside Mister Blood on a ruby-red diamond-patterned quilt that was worn down as thin as a lock of mourned beloved's hair. We listened with great reverence beings he was the wisest (and oldest) man either one of us knew in Goodlife.

"Were you a-feared?" Johnny Paul asked.

"Nope. Ma had always told me Psalms 34:7 say, *'The angel of the Lord encampth round about them that fear him, and delivereth them,'* and I knowed it be the Lord who would make providence on my behalf because the Bible said it. So, I fashioned my notions on holy words from Heaven, and the animals took me into their dens, caves, dells, cliffs and rocks, and waters until I was about twenty-one."

Again, Johnny Paul asked, "Were you a-feared though?"

"Not with the Lord looking down from Heaven on me, I weren't. I suspect that one lone timber wolf were an angel of mercy because she took me in first. I was taken by the way she wore her heart in her eyes. Then, she showed me how to fetch little critters to eat and what meat we brought in together kept my soul from spoiling."

Johnny Paul Russell's eyes rounded like dinner plates.

I looked down into the diamond-patterned quilt and saw how the flecks of ruby dusted it with cocoon images causing a hint of reflections to glitter in the sun which was reflecting in the bevel-set glass atop an old mahogany dresser. I glanced out an open window and a redbird flew into the arms of the flowering Judas whose limbs embraced the songbird like a woman would a man. The wind began to blow a warm breeze.

"The timber wolf made me as fat as a pup. We drank from the rivers unless they be with the breath of winter. We'd drink from soft snow under Macedonian skies moving on to the Hebrus River in midwinter. A lot of days I ate green herbs, sweet and bitter, from the Earth. But the *rivers* give us the most pleasure amid the dusty lilac skies—the rivers be filled with eternal life like those in the city of Goodlife."

"What words did you learn from the animals?" Johnny Paul asked.

Mister Blood cocked his head to the right a little and then told us, "Some animals speak inward then the sounds rise from deep within their being up on up into their throat giving birth to sounds brilliant and rare like gold air."

"*Really?*" I asked.

"It be true. Some sang as clear and as sweet as cherubs *seeking* peace while others could cause my heart to roll back upon itself in a stupor once their sounds peppered the air with jeweled teeth that could bite into the pure darkness."

"Mercy!" I cried.

Johnny Paul stood up. Then, he sat back down.

"More than once, their sounds united and caused an avalanche slamming my soul against the darkness of night leaving me burning from within for my Ma until the night nymphs and other spirits— some good; some evil—would come along and spur me along into the next day and on towards another night."

"Mister Blood, you going to tell us some animal words or not?" Johnny Paul asked.

I waited.

Cyrus Blood shook his head no and he reached into his front pocket and brought out a fistful of little, rough stones and rolled them against one another, opening and closing his hand on the lot of them as if he were trying to produce a divine spark, but nothing came forth.

"What you got there?" Johnny Paul asked.

He closed his hand and looked into the beveled mirror with a poet's eye.

I watched him close.

"The gray wolf told me, 'The way of words begins with Silence which overlooks the place where Bliss begins, and creation lies in limbo to the beckoning of the early light. And when the Sun opens Her mouth from the West like a glossy golden gate *only* then does mankind become at great risk because the secrets of the air can rain down heavy on him leaving him feeling lost until the eyes of Silence open and take pity and offer him the opening of the world—which goes like this, '*Once upon a rose, the blue overhanging dome that covers more than half of the Earth filled with music softer than the rain. But not like you and I know it, the music of all the animals and their voices painted the Earth with green trees, teal-blue seas, shimmering stars, crystal clear oceans, and tall, dark mountains and no one was poor because we were all the same like these here stones...*'"

Johnny Paul looked over at me, shocked.

"*We are living stones...* ripped from top to bottom until the fire comes."

I shrugged my shoulders at Johnny Paul.

Mister Blood stopped speaking and turned away from the beveled mirror which was now producing a double rainbow against the ruby-red quilt and us. He turned his hand palm side up and showed us the stones.

We bent forward and looked into his hands.

"These are diamonds in the rough," he stated.

Eyeing the stones with great suspicion, Johnny Paul told Mister Blood, "Them don't look like *real* diamonds to me."

Our friend looked at us with the face of a troubled heart and with tears rolling down his cheeks like silver moonbeams and asked, "Would one of you get me a cool drink of river water?"

Johnny Paul stood to his feet.

"I will," I offered and reached for a dark maroon metallic water pitcher that was already beading with clear droplets of water from the warm breeze.

He nodded once and wiped his eyes.

Beside the water pitcher were six colorful glasses—silver, emerald, lilac, gold, maroon, and amber.

What pretty glass

I reached for the amber one. I poured Mister Blood a glass of river water.

Johnny Paul reached with able hands and took it from me.

Then, I filled the emerald one for Johnny Paul and the lilac one about half-full for myself.

Putting the amber rim to his lips, Johnny Paul told him, "Cyrus, don't cry... Hear?"

"I can't help it—I miss my Ma when I go on sometimes...," he began.

The warm breeze turned cool and honey sweet when I took a sip from my glass.

"At night when I used to run with the Fawns and look into the stars I felt a jerking on my heart—a deep, unexplainable longing for her."

And, Reader, his face began to open.

"I feel that way when my Paw is out drinking and me and Maw and the twins—Judy and Jerry—are alone...," Johnny Paul interjected. He tapped the heels of his navy blue cowboy boots together three times then sighed before he mumbled, "Hot damn whiskey!"

I frowned.

"I never knowed what happened to my Ma. Night after night, I'd search all the eyes of the Piney Woods for hers. And when day would break, I'd run through Fields of Lush and say a prayer that the new day would bring her home. But it never happened—never. And like I said, only on a dark night could I feel her presence—but not her."

He took the amber glass from Johnny Paul and drank the river water all at once while holding on tight to it as if it were a Rosary bead.

"Powerfully bitter," he said into the glass.

Reaching for his emerald water glass, Johnny Paul mumbled, "The good Lord sure took care of you."

"Dear children of God, it be true."

"Mister Blood, do you think you are living out your destiny?" I asked.

Johnny Paul frowned.

Mister Blood thought for a minute and replied, "Could be so." He smiled with a burning blue sorrow at his own open face in the beveled mahogany mirror which was still hallowed by the doubled rainbow. He looked at us with a great gentleness in his eyes that clearly seeped out with every word he spoke *or remembered* about his life.

"Could be so," Johnny Paul echoed him.

"But, to tell you the truth, my life has been like a broken cistern that no one ever came along to fix."

I frowned.

All at once, his mood changed, and he began to weep at his own reflection in the mirror and the double rainbow faded away. Cyrus drew his hands to his face and covered it for a short time.

As plain as day, I saw an angel enter the room. It took a firm place by the door like the Guard of the Day, but not before placing a red rose inside the green Depression glass bowl amid the ten apples.

Johnny Paul ran over and put his hands on Mister Cyrus Blood.

Quite suddenly, my own hands felt just like Andromeda's hands when a determined stillness moved in on me like a strong chain leaving me feeling ever so dark and captured by the moment.

Being mindful of his tears, I was able to muster up the words. "Mister Blood, do you reckon if you try, that you can make sounds like gold air?"

Johnny Paul took his hands off him.

We waited.

He motioned for the amber glass. Earnestly, Johnny Paul held it out to him, but he did not take it. Instead, he gently traced its wet, amber rim with his rolled-up fist full of stones. Johnny Paul offered him the emerald glass but to no avail. He did manage a smile, though.

Then, calling to remembrance the unfeigned faith that was buried deep within him, Mister Blood nodded at us and closed both eyes, took in a *very* deep breath until a natural melody of notes rose through the air and passed over our heads all the while increasing with a sharp and an intense jubilation while pouring through and tumbling out of his earthly shell with the magic of a river dream causing Johnny Paul Russell to gently clasp his hands directly in front of him in midair as if he were capturing the soft glowing light of fireflies.

Now Reader, let it be known that Mister Cyrus Blood never even once opened his mouth. He only crackled and drummed and chaffed those uncut diamonds with a gentle yet *great* force in the crib of his Godly hand until right before our very eyes, he slowly opened up his hand and the rocks were no longer small and round and ugly, but radiating with a great rare brilliance *and* beholding to our eyes with a glistening golden-white stream of light that filled the room until it began to illuminate back onto his blue face causing his eyes to glisten and radiate like two diamonds of ice banded with pure, flaming peace.

And, only then, did the angel leave the room.

CLARA STRAW

Redemption

Redemption is the only word that comes to mind when I think of Clara Straw. At least, that was *what* her step-momma, Amaryllis, had in mind on Clara's thirteenth birthday on February 14, 1875, when she let Clara share a seat with her Uncle Beryl for the first time since April 1, 1867. Clara and Uncle Beryl rode together all the way from Selma, Alabama, to Goodlife, Mississippi, to watch them bury Clara's Maw, Azuerine Underwood. That's when her troubles began.

Eyes like a harvest moon, Clara Straw asked me, "Myra Boone, you ever rode on a train track?"

Watching her close while she sat comfortably in the corner of a box-like room she'd made into a screened-in front porch, I replied, "Not that I recall."

Brushing the naked air lightly with her right hand, she said as if to warn me, "Be glad of it."

"Why?" I asked her.

Face glowing like a child, she informed me, "I was five my first time—when my *real* Maw died. Exactly thirteen when my next Maw died. Neither time had a happy ending."

"Oh," was all I knew to say.

"I was fat as a kitten and soft and *unaware* too. Who ain't at thirteen?"

I continued to watch her, close, but didn't speak. She had jet-black hair. She told me that she had dyed it with store-bought shoe polish and homemade bleach for years. And her fingers were stained yellow from cigars and home-grown tobacco. She wore a rose-gold band on her right index finger and had a pretty but baggy lilac dress on. It fitted her quite well except down around the arms there was darker color of purple material that resembled a thin, ribbon-like shawl that hung down her sides like two streamers, making her two naked arms look like the thin stems of a rose bush. Both of her arms were marred and lashed with blue-black scars that made me think of a slew of broken veins. She'd assured me that the lashes were made by a red-orange mule whip *only in* the spirit of love.

Slowly, and with great suspicion, I asked, "Miss Straw, what happens on a train track?"

"Nothing much. If you can count, you got it made, but since I couldn't, all I could do was gaze out the windows and watch the pine trees pass. The end of the ride is what is bad—at least in my case," she informed me while drumming her stained fingers on the floor.

"Why?"

"That's when I found out that my step-Maw had done gone and sold me to Mister Eli Peters—who was sixty years old *and then some* when I first laid down in his bed," she told me.

My eyes widened, and my heart fell down into my stomach.

"Mister Peters like me a lot—I could tell. But I hated his damn guts!" she sounded out.

"Ah, ha," was all I could think to say.

Clara raised her left eyebrow while winking with her right eye at me before she said, "I baked for him all sorts of desserts though. Mister Peters' favorites were the ones I made with nutmeg. He never knew what hit him 'till it was too late!"

"Ah."

She smiled wryly at me. I smiled back, feeling uneasy in her presence.

"Why if it wasn't for Brother Jim Roberts coming around with that little Margie Anne once a week since she was old enough to tote a sack from Blue's Corner Store, and The People of the Way feeding me scraps for years—why I'd of dried up like a sack of black bricks and chicken bones a long time ago!"

I smiled.

She considered her words then asked, "Know what Mister Peters did to me?"

"No," I said, piercing my bottom lip with my eye teeth.

"I'll tell you what Mister Peters did to me—for starters, he made me have pretty near three miscarriages before my nineteenth birthday with that red-orange mule whip in the cold waters of Taylor Creek!"

"What's a miscarriage?" I asked her, knowing how freezing cold Taylor Creek stayed all year round.

Switching her rose-gold band from her right index finger to her left middle finger, she told me, "A dead—well, a baby born dead or such."

I frowned.

"Yes, I could have had me three youngins' to keep me company in my old days of 100 if it weren't for him—*afflicting* me like he did—in my young good days," she told the sky.

My eyes widened, lost for words.

"It was the most awful thing you can even think of!"

"I suppose so."

"It's so! Nothing be any worse than pulling a baby out of yourself as limp as an old bloody rag."

I frowned.

"Then the crazy old man never let me sleep!"

"Why not?"

"Dogged if I can figure it out to this very day other than he was crazy as a Betsy bug from drinking all that corn whiskey he was right fond of and always sanging some little verse that went something like this, *I'm re-deem-ed by the blood divine—glory, glory Christ is mine, Christ is mine. All to Him I now resign—I have been re-deem-ed!*

She threw me a quizzical look.

"Mercy!"

"Sang it all the time—for years! *Said* it made him *happy* to sang. Mister Peters had had four other wives before me. Listen, I ain't for certain that I was his *wife*, but I knowed I *belonged* to him 'cause I still got the paper." Clara stopped talking and looked me directly in the face and asked, "Miss Myra, can you read?"

"I can."

"Well, *good Gaw'd Almighty!* Will you let me go in yonder and get it right quick?"

"Go on."

She left me alone on the front porch to think that being able to read was a good thing until she returned with a yellow stained piece of paper. She shoved it in my face but not before I noticed the little serpentine glint in her eyes. I was glad to see it only held one sentence and that the print was good. I was thankful it was not in real — cursive — writing.

"I never lost heart nor wavered in my obedience. I knowed someone would come along someday and be able to read the piece of paper to me. Would you just let me get comfortable before you tell me what it says?"

I waited.

Flopping her old black body down on the corner of her screen porch near an assortment of trinkets and dolls and marbles and see-through glass crystals and beads that reminded me of a child's playhouse only there was no wooden box to hold them all, Clara Straw told me, "Read the truth to this old Negro woman."

I read, *"In the name of God, on this Saint's Day, February 14, 1875, I sell for the sum one one-hundred pennies one virgin snowdrop (age 13), Clara Straw, to Mister Eli Peters to keep as his slave until he deems to set her free or upon his death. Signed: Amaryllis."*

Eyes black as a raven, she echoed me, "In the name of God —,"

When a light breeze began to blow, a woodsy-honey smell entered the porch.

When I looked up, Clara was smiling and holding a small chocolate-colored doll that looked like an old man dressed in overalls and a yellow cap. She was in deep thought, twirling the doll between the fingers of her right hand.

"What you got there?"

Eyeing the man doll while still mulling over her thoughts, she said, "It's a Mommet of *my* Mister Peters."

Seeing the road through a crack in the screen door, I frowned.

Shaking the Mommet, she told me, "So *now* I am re-deem-ed, beings Mister Peters is gone."

We both bent our ears to hear a faint train whistle in the distance.

"I suppose."

"Miss Myra, it's a good thing you come along to read the piece of paper to me, or else I'd of never knowed the truth. I thank you kindly."

I smiled, placing the yellow stained piece of paper on the floor while reaching for a rusty, silver cake pan that gave off the odor of nutmeg to anchor the paper from any movement whatsoever.

Clara switched her rose-gold band back to her right index finger and calmly stated, "All my fingers are the same size—except for my little fingers."

I frowned.

She began to laugh and laugh like a hyena before she broke into song, "*Clara Straw is re-deem-ed by the blood divine—glory, glory Christ is hers, Christ is hers. All to Them she now resigns—for she has been re-deem-ed...*"

A brilliant red-orange sun was setting in the eastern sky. When I looked out the screen door directly into it, I could see that it was beginning to slowly turn like a fireball against a cloudless Mississippi azure blue sky while Miss Straw hummed her little tune like I wasn't even in the room. Soon she pointed off to the side of the house at a cemetery with a little yellow fence hugging eight cross-like wooden markers. She threw me a smile, and with her right index finger she thumped a series of see-through, crystal-like beads—saffron, lilac, lime, aqua, peach, pink, gray, and amber—out a little hole in the screen that was directly in front of her, all the while humming and chanting in tongues.

Slowly, I rose and slipped on out the screen door determined to stay shed of the train tracks, but I found myself just having to look back because I was ashamed of myself for not properly saying good-bye. And when I did, Clara Straw was up on her bare feet standing on the front steps of her box-like porch still singing her song. She was waving her naked arms at me, and they were turning like a windmill while the wind blew the purple streams of material against her pretty, baggy lilac dress dreamily against the deep, blue-black scars made by a red-orange mule whip *only in* the spirit of love. The sun smiled down on her rose-gold band, making it sparkle like a star against her old black, lone body. A train whistle echoed in the distance as she twirled that Mommet between the fingers of her left hand. In her right hand, Miss Straw shook a silver cake pan like a tambourine and sang in a little pinched voice, "*Glory, glory Christ is mine Christ is mine.*"

THE NAKED MAN

Faith

"**J**esus—*you dirty little dog, you!*" the Reverend Jade Styron, naked as a jaybird, cried out from his Hollywood bed while sending everyone in the room a pleasurable smile.

"Oh, my God in Heaven," Camille whispered, taking me by the hand as we walked straight past their only girl, Midge, and on towards Jade's ash-blue naked body.

He looked like he'd been in the middle of a volcano for at least a thousand years or more. The color of his skin was smoky in some spots while red like a pomegranate in others, but it clearly held a hue of ash. His arms were skinless except for the upper shoulders which, strangely enough, still held just a tad of pinkness to them on what little skin had not been completely gnawed off—by Jade and time—or perhaps rotted off. His lips were a coal gray with a tinge of scarlet in their center.

"Camille! Tell Midge to get me a fresh sheet to cool my skin. Hear?" he cried out.

Camille, his *beloved* of forty-eight years, dutifully obeyed his sudden command and said, "Midge, oh, Midge! Git in here with your Daddy a clean set of sheets as fast as your tiny legs will carry you!"

"I'm a-coming," was all the girl said, dragging her feet and heading towards the back of the house. She was considerably crippled in her legs.

"Reverend Styron, will you try to be *nice* because Myra Boone just come in to see you for just a spell? She brung you some fruit," Camille told him in a kind voice.

His voice was throaty like a wild animal, "Is that so?"

"Hello, Reverend Styron," I finally said, feeling cut to the bone before he even said one word to me. I laid the bag of fruit on his walnut dresser beneath its oval diamond-dusted mirror.

"Hell!" he said laughingly at the patchy blue wall that held hundreds of lilywhite vertical lines directly to his left.

I felt his only word sting my heart like a sudden blow of destruction.

Camille said in a most soothing voice, "Jade, you be nice, now. Hear?"

"The end is near! Why'd *you* come, *Neighbor?*" was all he spit out my way.

Dragging both feet, Midge entered the room and handed him two sheets folded like grave clothes. One sheet was milky white like a wet snowflake and the other one yellow like a bright ray of sunshine. He proceeded to stand; then he neatly laid the sunny sheet across his Hollywood bed and lay down while covering his nakedness with the milky one. He sat straight up, erect-like, and smiled at the lot of us before crying out, "Son-of-a-Bitch is what I feel like!"

Midge rolled her eyes at Camille who up and left the room heading straight for the kitchen, leaving me and Midge alone with Jade.

Midge whispered to me, "Myra, don't believe him. He's lying as usual."

All I could think bout was his naked body though. But I managed to nod to her.

Jade smiled at me, and I saw a little serpentine glint in his eyes.

Although nakedness reminds some folks of a newborn baby and others of great beauty, I could see that it was *mysterious* and ancient and deep—at least to my eyes. Jade himself was like a dark menagerie of sorts is all I know to say. And his naked body seemed to be suspended in his Hollywood bed by some hidden dark chains, which were slowly disappearing around his nakedness as if to soon choke the life out of him.

"Is he in pain?" I asked Midge.

"Naw. His nerves are long gone," she told me, shaking her head.

My eyes widened.

Midge rolled her eyes at an open window when a cool honey breeze joined us.

Neither of us said a word.

With his neck stretching up to the ceiling four feet off his shoulders and scaring me far worse than anything had ever scared me before that day Jade cried out, "I am the most *fateful* preacher in the history of the Soso, Mississippi's Church of the Only Ones! And you all know it. Tell me it ain't so—tell me it ain't so! Tell me I didn't feed *my* flock, wisely—tell me!"

I felt that I would soon faint, but I didn't when he cried out even louder, "*Jesus—you dirty little dog, you!*"

ed the room with a tray of silver cups of iced tea

Camille ı sprigs of fresh mint. "Now, look what I brought for

graced yra, would you like sugar or *Sweet 10*?"

our ³d, eyeing the patchy blue wallpaper as its lily white

ɩes began to twist and move like twinkling bells right

host.

ɩ, looking at the silver cups.

' Midge said, heading for the walnut dresser. She picked

ɔf fruit and turned it upside down on the glass top in front

ɩamond-dusted oval.

Sugar!" Jade cried out, shaking his bare shoulders at her.

"Now, now, now, Jade Styron, *sugar* is one thing you don't need,"
Camille said in that soothing voice of hers.

"Bitch, go straight to hell!" he told her.

Camille ignored him.

Dragging her feet, Midge left the room.

"Reverend Styron, take the *Sweet 10*," she advised him.

He looked timid for the first time since I'd arrived.

Midge slowly entered the room with a pear knife.

Jade watched her closely.

She took a pear from the dresser and began to p

before she took a sip of her iced-tea.   *ut not*

"Tutti-frutti!" Jade said, eyeing the pear.

Midge set her eyes straight on him like two flints.

Camille smiled and reached for the bag and took out an

"Now, Jade, *dear*, won't you tell Myra Boone about the Holy G

Midge choked on her iced-tea.

Jade's eyes widened, but he soon sent me a sweet smile.

"Reverend Styron, did you hear me?" Camille asked him.

"I got it in the fire is all I know," he told me, eyeing the ceiling.

Midge smiled and looked straight at me, then nodded before saying with a cheery smile beneath her voice, "He's telling the truth now."

I watched her close, wondering why she'd even bothered to speak.

"I am," he stated.

Camille grinned like a court jester.

I waited like a pigeon.

Camille gave a little whistle of "Way Down in Dixie."

"My deacons come out to the house and were aimed to take Midge out and bullwhip her on account of her running with that Stringer boy from the Union Universal Church in Soso. That's how I ended up in the fire," he said, sipping his iced-tea, but not before removing the sprig of mint. He smiled at it and threw it against the oval mirror.

Camille dutifully got up and removed it and used the elbow of her dress sleeve to shine the oval.

I frowned.

"I keep a memory book, so I don't forget nothing," Midge put in, reaching beneath her seat and bringing back a pretty little book with a cloth-like cover the color of scarlet.

Jade gazed at her while looking lost in thought.

"Nothing," she repeated to herself.

Camille said, "Honey, you can show Myra later. Let your Daddy tell her about the Holy Ghost." She threw the orange into the air, and then she caught it.

Midge bounced her head a little, then smoothed down her skirt before confessing, "The Devil—he knowed what my weakness was just like he knowed what Solomon's was—is all I got to say!"

Camille nodded and began to peel her orange with her fingers.

Jade came back to himself and gave her the evil eye.

"Midge, *honey*, let Daddy talk now," Camille told her daughter.

Guiltily, Midge looked down at her pear knife.

"I got tears all in my eyes," Jade said, sarcastically. He spilled some of his iced-tea between his legs, then looked down at himself and smiled while boxing at his instrument with his right hand.

"*Daddy* blames me," Midge told me then just above a whisper she added, "*Who else to blame?*"

I frowned.

"Jesus Christ would have sent you a snow-white bull to court if you'd just a-waited on Him," Jade told her and licked the top of his right hand.

"Now, now, now, Reverend Styron, tell Miss Myra Boone about your reward," Camille encouraged him.

Midge rolled her eyes at them.

Smiling at an orange wedge, Camille said, "This is a sweet one."

"No man could have been any more god-like in Goodlife if he'd of been shot straight out of a star nor a listening sky than *my* Bolt Stringer!" Midge cried out in a defensive voice.

"He was a poor man's hope is all that Stringer boy was," Jade shot back at her.

"I loved Bolt—with all my heart! And no one would let me have any peace about it the minute the truth was let out!" Midge screamed out.

"What truth? That God's *only* child is a Blackie lover?!" Jade screamed at his daughter.

"You ain't God!" Midge screamed back then added, "And I ain't His *only* child either!"

Camille stood up and proclaimed, "Stop it!"

"Hell, look at her—she ain't learnt nary thang yet!" Jade said, shooting Midge a sharp long look along with a cool stream of bitterness in his voice before spitting out the words, "Like the first Day and the last Night of the year is what you two looked like meeting in the Piney Woods of Goodlife!"

Finally, I spoke up again and said, "Reverend Styron, tell me about the Holy Ghost."

Everyone grew silent.

Jade's neck stretched four feet off his shoulders and scared me slam to death.

Seemingly, no one seemed to consider it the least bit unusual just before he once again spit out the words, "*Jesus—you dirty little dog, you!*"

Scared, I stood up to go.

"Oh, Myra, *please* don't go—none of our neighbors ever come around to see us anymore. *Please*, stay," Midge said in a most pleading voice.

When I looked at her, I could see that her eyes were filled with heavy tears, making me feel sadder for her than her folks who were clearly in a shameful fix.

When Jade came back to himself, I sat back down.

Midge looked relieved and, strangely enough, happy.

"*Remember the blood*," Camille whispered to an orange wedge.

"Midge was our Firstborn—," Jade began.

Camille interrupted with, "Our *one* born."

I looked over towards Midge who was now neatly peeling her pear and putting the strips of skins into her front pocket.

"I begged God to free Camille from her long night of horror and to shed Grace all about Goodlife and this house until she was freed up that cold spring night with not a soul on God's green earth to deliver her."

I frowned.

Midge mumbled, "Bolt Stringer was *truly* my *only* reason for living. Our love was like shining ivory. Bolt even taught me how to skin a deer."

I was beginning to notice that the longer Jade talked, the louder his voice grew like he was preaching before a crowd.

"When the deacons come that night, I thought for sure they'd come to tell me the results of the vote, if you want to know the truth about it," he said.

"*Vote?*" I asked.

Midge looked up like she was hearing his words for the first time. Her lips were parted as if she might whistle a tune.

Camille crossed her legs. Then, she uncrossed them.

Jade continued on with, "Yes, vote! My members had all stayed after prayer meeting one Wednesday night and took a vote on my reinstatement for two more years. Now, they had had some *concerns* beings not nary a soul had gotten healed let alone had received the Holy Ghost since, oh, about a year or so before their election if my mind is clear enough to think back on it."

Again, Midge set her eyes straight on him like two flints.

Camille stated, "God is faithful though."

"Why do you think that God calls His children?" Jade asked me like I knew.

I shrugged my shoulders.

Midge began to thumb through her memory book. When she stopped, she brushed over a page with her index finger, and her lips were moving but no sound came.

Jade Styron began to preach, "To exhort them toward the Truth and, of course, the *Blood*, and the well—." He stopped and turned toward his only girl and said, "Tell, Myra Boone, Midge, tell her what the voice of God Almighty says to those who ain't Believers when they try to steal one of His children!"

Midge looked up from reading her memory book with a colorless face.

Camille said, "Midge?"

"Son-of-a-Bitch!" Midge proclaimed.

Jade gave us a shocked look.

I frowned.

"See how *she* is?" he asked his wife.

"Still, *she* ain't settled—yet," Camille said, looking at Midge with regret before saying, 'Honor thy mother and thy father: that thy days may be long upon the land which the Lord thy God giveth thee.' Honey, remember that memory verse from Sunday School? The one you wrote a thousand times in your memory book. The first commandment with promise."

The fifth commandment that the Lord God gave Moses—Exodus 20:12, I thought.

"You are a liar!" Midge screamed and threw her memory book at the mirror. It shattered to bits like a million diamonds.

"She's as wicked as the Devil!" Jade told Camille who only shook her head.

Filled with terror, I held onto my neck as if it might stretch.

Midge turned to me and calmly said, "Daddy told *me* diff-er-ent was all I was going to say."

The pear knife fell to the floor.

I clenched my teeth in disbelief.

It was Jade who spoke, "Azazel."

I held onto my neck even tighter.

He bleated like a goat.

Screaming an unholy scream, "Auauauhahahaha! It ain't so! That was never the truth!" Midge looked all around the room.

Camille smoothed her dress down.

I bit at the inside of my jaws with my back teeth.

"Myra, Daddy swore when I was born that a heavenly Host of angels sang words of Grace in Momma's ears to rid her of the horrors of my coming, which could only mean that no earthly man, only a *heavenly* man, would the good Lord send my way—in God's appointed time—could I even consider loving not a Blackie," Midge told me, chewing on her bottom lip.

I said nothing.

"My snow White sheep not my Blackie lovers will know my voice, and when I come, they will surely see *my* shining face in the Day of Glory not in the Night of Hades," Jade went on like a mad dog quoting bits of Scripture until he twisted his tongue.

Midge stood and asked her father, "You let them kill *my* Bolt! *Didn't you?!* You knowed I loved Bolt Stringer with all my heart and soul! Bolt Stringer was my Beloved!"

He ignored her question and proclaimed, "To receive the Holy Ghost—you must have a ready mind and be willing to let go of filthy lucre—repent, confess, and believe, and *not* turn from, *but* towards, the Cross."

Camille sighed.

"*I* was an example to my flock. I took on *my* afflictions like the chief Shepherd should. Now, I am being made perfect like Christ Jesus... And I will receive *my* crown in Glory as soon as the Master calls out *my* name!" He paused to smile with great satisfaction before saying, "*My* words are as good as the streets of gold in Goodlife!"

Quickly, Midge emptied her pocket of the pear peelings.

Jade stood up from his Hollywood bed stark naked.

I closed my eyes fast, and then I slowly opened them.

Midge reached down for the pear knife.

Camille held her breath and threw a hopeful look my way.

"Let's pray," was all I knew to say, and a sweet, rosy smell entered the room.

But it was too late. Midge lunged at her earthly father with the knife. Then much to my surprise, Reverend Jade Styron reached out to her and snatched the knife out of her hands and gave us all a wicked smile before thrusting its silver blade gallantly into his neck, not once like you'd think, but over and over again as if to mutilate a member of the Body of Christ until the floor began to fill profusely with the color of scarlet like the cover of Midge's beloved memory book.

Like the stillness of peace, the diamond-like sprinkles of crimson blood shot against the yellow and white bed sheets until it trickled over to join the broken bits of glass. Camille and Midge wailed in another tongue unfamiliar to me as the vertical lines amid the patchy blue walls began to close in on her earthly father's ashen nakedness like chains of dancing pearls.

It was me who managed to utter, "Dear Lord God, have mercy on us."

Then, just as the Day met with the Night in the Piney Woods of Goodlife, the Reverend Jade Styron's naked body jerked three times and slithered to the floor and was made perfect.

ANANIAS

Glory

One azure Sunday Margie Anne Roberts and I went to visit a crippled old man named Ananias.

"Ever drifted through the bar-like boles of Eden amid the firmament?" Ananias' words filled the room like a sculpture fills the stone.

Margie Anne gave me a furious frown and pursed her lips when I said, "No."

"You mean the dark?" Margie Anne asked.

"Nope. Dark ain't got any vaulting hues to it. It just is. The dark doesn't move."

"What do you mean then?" I asked.

"The undimmed air of the true earth above us that is tormented by the moaning flow of wind in the gray of morning. It be so strong and powerful that I've even felt it pierce my earthly shell with its black mist low creeping, dragging down before it slams the soul against itself!" he went on.

Margie Anne winced.

I looked out an open window and saw two slender catbirds scratching in some dead leaves for bugs.

I got my nerve up and asked, "Ananias, have you?"

"Of course, Myra Boone! How'd you thank I got my spine snapped in two this way?" He motioned for a bottle of homemade pink liniment that was sitting directly in the center of a pine bookcase before whispering, "In the Garden."

Margie Anne took in a deep breath then let it out.

I looked from him to the catbirds that were mimicking a much older voice in the Piney Woods of Goodlife.

Ananias hung his black head sorely low.

Margie Anne got up to get the bottle of pink liniment for him.

"Don't burn your'n hands!" he cried out.

"Ananias, I don't aim to put it *on you*! I'm only handing it *to you*," she told him.

Ananias looked up at her from his old wooden wheelchair which sported a jaunty little American flag. He gave a toothless smile and pulled at his snow-white beard and then reached into a tiny homemade, bright green cloth purse that was dotted with hundreds of daises and pulled out a glowing Bible. He gave it the once-over before returning it to the cloth purse.

I looked around the room and saw three tarnished silver picture shells hanging on the wall over a single army cot and felt an ache in my heart for my folks.

Margie Anne pushed her thick glasses back up onto her nose and looked around for a place to sit.

I hate the smell of liniment.

Ananias made a motion towards a black, glossy three-blade fan and said, "Will one of you plug in my fan? I'm feeling flushed."

Margie Anne obliged him.

The fan made an unstable sound at first. Then it hummed like a bee. The little American flag began to blow briskly in its secure place from the back of his wooden wheelchair.

In the saddest voice I'd ever heard, Ananias told us this, "I was knee deep in the firmament and feeling like a beggar on my knees with the fragrant dark hanging all around me wanting to break into

Day's early light that was trying to rise, naturally, on out of Eden. Suddenly, the Earth's Dome opened up and showed me the water's blue, which is the shade of thought, and shocked my mind into a prism of white, pure light—*sun-dipped*—if you please. Just then one of life's unexpected explosions came along and snapped my back in two and shattered my nerves to hell and back, leaving me defeated in this wheelchair for the rest of my earthly life!"

Clapping her hands twice, Margie Anne cried out, "My Lord a-mercy!"

Feeling lost for words, I asked, "What did you do then?"

Margie Anne fell back into a high-back rocker.

"With a searching heart, I asked God to place within me everything I'd ever need to live in Eden—now Goodlife. This was a stupid thing as any to have asked for—beings I already had it all," he told us.

He pointed to the three-tarnished silver empty picture shells, then to the single army cot.

"Of all things," Margie Anne mumbled.

I shrugged my shoulders at no one.

Ananias held onto the bottle of pink liniment like an angel holding a column of rose-gold as he told us, "Yep, I was born walking in the light of the living without corruption or lust. God *tried* to reveal

Himself to me, but I turned a deaf ear to His voice. In the shadow of my own mind, I tuned God out."

I didn't know what to say to that.

Rocking in her chair, Margie Anne said, "Do tell."

He slid his date-brown eyes over her way, then thumped once at the daisies on his little cloth purse.

I looked out the window and saw that the catbirds were now sitting in a golden pear tree and eating on its first fruits.

"Before the earthly city of Goodlife, I remember living among the dragons, fire, hair, snow, *and* vapor and all deeps where the sun and the moon used to cry out to my ears amid the blue stars of light. Back then the wind blew so strong that it spoke words of freedom and not violent storms of destruction like it do nowadays."

Margie Anne crossed her legs and began to kick the naked air with her right foot.

"I'll never forget the fruitful trees and the hills where the woods were loaded with creeping things and flying fowl that made sounds like cupped-trumpets," he told us.

I asked, "Ananias, you ever seen any Saints before?"

"Not in Eden, I didn't."

Kicking the naked air with a great force of energy, Margie Anne interjected, "Where then?"

"Between Heaven and earth is where—dropping down, that is."

He opened his pink liniment, and a sharp, piney smell filled the air.

Margie Anne sat up as straight as a board and said, "Tell us more, please."

He cleared his throat and coughed once before asking, "You won't think me crazy like the rest of the town?"

"Of course not!" we said in perfect unison.

He reached into his shirt pocket and brought back a little sprayer of sorts and dropped it smartly into the cloudy pink liquid.

We listened.

"In the middle of the earth, there is a *deep* neon purple space where the souls lie in wait until their names are called. Some call it Glory—some call it Rest. I ain't narrow-minded enough to rule anything out beings I aim to tell you girls that I ain't for sure what God is up to in His just *and secret* counsel. And He ain't known for deceiving folk, let alone telling more than we *now* frail ones have a need to know about. In other words, God ain't revealed it to me, but I've been there."

Margie Anne looked over the rim of her glasses at him, but she didn't utter a sound.

The catbirds began to sing sweetly outside the window, all the while pecking on the gold pears in the brightness of the sun that had singled them out like a moving picture.

I asked, "Are the Saints happy there or not?"

Giving his neck a sure shot of pink liniment, he told us, "Being among the first to fall, I can only speak this much Truth to you girls: The Saints be in the company of angels and beyond the reach of the Enemy—Death—and the Two were in the beginning amid the pure and white-white light."

With true Roberts' concern, Margie Anne asked him, "What I would like to know is how you remember that *far back?*"

"Girls, I may not have my back to hold me up, but I do have my mind," he told us. I nodded knowing he was speaking the truth as he believed it to be.

Margie Anne put her thumb in her mouth and began to chew on her thumbnail.

The wind visited the room like an invited guest but failed to stay.

"Sometimes I feel like I'm walking to sleep when the memories snake into my mind and blacken it with thoughts that God has left me."

Margie Anne gasped.

"Especially when the town's people laugh and make fun of an old Negro like me. Some of the children even kick my wheels and throw pennies, rocks, and sand at me. I can't do nary a thing about it—being paralyzed like I be in some places and without family or friends only me neighbors to help me towards the house."

I ran over to him, and Margie did the like.

"Ananias, we'll see to it that they leave you be—from here on out," I promised him and put my arms around him as best I could.

"From here on out!" Margie Anne echoed me.

He hung his neck down like a great yoke of sorrow had been placed around it.

I bowed my head and prayed for Grace. Then, I looked over on a little cherry glass-topped coffee table and saw an unusual flower with petals that seemed to be hanging on for dear life.

Pointing to the potted plant, I asked, "Ananias, what kind of flower is that? Is it a witch hazel?"

With a great effort, he lifted his neck and gave a bright smile.

Margie Anne walked over to the cherry table for a closer look.

"It is a windflower with petals of white chalcedony and leaves of gold," he told us.

"Oh, my goodness," Margie Anne said into the leaves of gold.

"I'm good at growing things—it's my gift," he stated.

I walked over to the windflower. And sure enough it bore petals of white chalcedony and leaves of pure gold.

"My gift is the one thing I managed to hang onto," he muttered and clicked his tongue once.

"Lilacs are my favorite," Margie Anne told him. She began to blow lightly at the windflower as if it was a lighted candle.

"Mine be yellow violets," Ananias put in, then uttered soft and low, "*Ve-ri-tas.*"

Shortly, I asked, "Margie Anne, what are you doing now?"

"Saying a prayer," she replied.

I rolled my eyes and asked, "Why?"

"What else would you do in the presence of such a glorious plant?"

He took out his Bible. It was glowing.

Outside, I could hear the catbirds singing with many voices like a wind song. I closed my eyes and said a prayer, too. And when I opened them, I saw that Ananias was desperately trying to stand up from his old wooden wheelchair. The sight of his struggle brought tears to my eyes, causing me to squint even tighter and pray as long and hard as my mind would let me while trying to imagine what it would be like to walk to sleep and live among the angels and the Saints amid the blue stars of light in a purple neon space in the earth called Glory where the Enemy called Death could not touch me or any of my family ever again.

I searched my mind for the Earth's Dome to show me the water's blue that held my shade of thought until I heard something hit the floor. When I opened my eyes, I saw that the little American flag had fallen from its secure place in the wooden wheelchair and was lying on the floor.

Margie Anne opened her eyes, and like a turtledove, she flew over to the colorful flag and picked it up and began to twirl it like a twigged laurel of praise between the fingers of her right hand to the outside echoes of the poetic catbird's song.

And when Ananias took his last breath, fell to the floor, and entered Glory, the glow on his Bible grew dimmer and dimmer until it was no more.

SUNSHINE BLACK

Death

"Myra Boone, never be a light unto your own self," Ambrose Twain said, with sapphire blue eyes of mistrust as we followed a path into the night garden of Goshen towards Peace Stream.

I nodded at him while eyeing a horizontal sundial.

"Do you think me *old*?" Ambrose asked.

I gave him a tight smile.

"Never mind," he said in a releasing voice and showed me a closed jackknife.

Ambrose Twain stood tall and erect amid the yellow azaleas that were starting to close their topaz satin blossoms under the faint blue twilight of Goshen. His slightly pointed ears gave him a fawn-like charm beneath his coal black hair. He reached down and picked up a veined stone, brought it to his purple-black lips, and breathed a kiss onto it. Then he threw it at the horizontal sundial's Roman numerals like a God-bound stone meant to awaken the dead.

"Ambrose, if you want to know the truth—I don't know what to think of you," I told him.

He stroked his cheek which held the hue of a Tahitian black pearl but didn't speak.

Realizing what I had said, I smiled without fear.

He moaned.

"Where did you come from before living in Goshen?"

He looked at me with the privileged eyes of someone divinely guided and asked, "My truth?"

"Of course."

"Ophir. I was washed ashore years ago by the gleaming waves of a silver-blue moonlit ocean while apes and peacocks searched for their next meal. What I remember about my birth is—"

I interrupted him, "You remember *your own birth?*"

Ambrose gently set his sapphire blue eyes on me and said, "I do. I was awakened in a little hollow of sand lit by the moon glow as the silver-blue water licked my face, which was quite alluring even as a baby. A flock of peacocks found an open space to swim around me while apes watched from the shoreline terrified of the ocean. A rosary of black pearls was found around my little bowl of sand. My birth was announced by a loud burst of silver-blue water that filled the air like a giant gold statue crashing to the ground."

I took in a deep breath and bent my ear to listen while I watched his beautiful black face and wondered why some men never marry. He began to make cradling gestures with his arms. And even though he was a spirit, he looked like a young boy holding onto his first tomorrow.

"One peacock, eyes flecked with gold and silver, reached into my mouth with its short beak, and took out a white pearl, notwithstanding the spectrum of the moon's light. The peacocks and the apes cried tears like yesterday's rain because I was to be alone — forever."

"Like an empty ocean?"

He nodded.

"Forever?"

Again, he nodded.

For a moment, we were as silent as twin gray shadows in the soft blue twilight of Time. I looked over towards the Goshen night garden and saw a sleeping swan begin to bury its head into its feathers while a new moon rose over Peace Stream.

"When were you born?" I asked.

"The day after tomorrow," he replied.

I gave him a puzzled look.

Reaching for my hand, Ambrose stroked my cheek and gently said, "Ashes of rose—would you like to see my heart light?"

I smiled.

He watched me close.

Knowing he meant no harm nor to allure me with anything other than meaningful words, I answered, "I suppose so."

Releasing my hand, he began to walk away from me towards the night garden.

I waited.

He bade me to come.

The moon turned full, then gold.

I obeyed his gesture.

Again, he offered me his hand. I took it, and together we walked into a night garden of glowing flowers.

The night garden and Peace Stream were nested by a gold fence that had silver scrolls welded into every other sixth bar like shields of

Judean armor. Embedded in the fence were amethyst and onyx stones which sparkled like purple and black diamonds amid the moon's glow. Purple ferns and blue roses were sleeping along the gold fence. I saw lavender jade vases, empty and begging to caress a flower—any flower—in a supernatural loveliness that surrounded us. I looked through an opening in the trees and saw an arch of ivy that held three sleepy birds twittering delicate notes amongst themselves. The rose-scented wind entered my mind like a whispering prayer. While we walked on oval Italian marble stones, the junipers slept all around us.

Ambrose Twain squeezed my hand.

I smiled at the aura of his black face.

Again, he sighed.

I looked up.

He was floating more than walking.

The night sky above us gemmed with blue stars full of silent, deep mystical lure. I looked about me to see lilacs, mimosas, and yellow azaleas all sleeping near Peace Stream. There were three tall, young, white-skinned birches lit up like three candles in the moonlight while older dark-skinned trees tossed their arms free and glad across the stream's water.

With an essence of truth that even I cannot describe, Ambrose told me, "I am a survivor of many centuries."

I looked into his sapphire blue eyes with bewilderment and saw that they were now filled with pure light. Without warning, they closed as if weighted down by centuries of Time. I felt a sharp tang of frost in the night air wrap around my legs.

A sleeping swan stirred.

"You mean like in Bible times?" I asked.

He shook his head yes then no.

"In On—where the Creator closed the doors to the streets and their sounds became muffled. The daughters of music became quiet. The birds sang soft and low. Strong men fought with the great fierceness of lions. Where the sun, the moon, and the stars never once turned to darkness, nor did the clouds return after the rain until words of truth were spoken like, 'Anger and rebellion can be transmitted into a thing of beauty. Without love there is no beauty in life.'"

"Ambrose, have you ever been in love before?"

"Without love, all becomes hell—even eternity." he told me then uttered something unintelligible.

I stopped walking when two white rabbits crossed our path and hopped into the yellow azaleas before zipping onto a pile of white marble-like rocks.

Nodding while pointing over towards the mouth of Peace Stream, he said, "The young conies take refuge in the rocks."

When I saw a tiny lantern giving off an ice-blue flame into an oblong beveled glass that topped the earth beneath my feet, again, I asked, "Ambrose, have you ever been in love before?"

"Not with a *woman*—" I had a funny feeling run through me until he said, "With words and Constellations—with the constellations of words have I loved."

I frowned. "How can that be?"

"With Sunshine Black's words—that is. Come, I'll show you."

I felt my heart open.

"She was a writer from New Orleans and more beautiful than Andromeda," he told me. The moon's glow began to dance off Peace Stream, bathing his eyes in its aura, causing them to gleam like two blue diamonds. He turned and gave me a considerable long look before the cold wind of reality slapped me in the face, reminding me that the worst thing in the world is for a body to be alone and without someone to love. I looked towards the ice-blue burning light for warmth but found none.

He caught my glance and said, "Uriel keeps the flame lit. Look into the glass."

I did and saw a beautiful Negro woman who appeared to be sleeping in a lighted coffin. Her head bore a wreath of silver and bronze leaves that were intertwined around her coal-black long ringlets hair. Her eyelids gleamed with tiny bits of crushed emeralds. And the color of her skin was a coppery bronze. Her cheeks were perfect and intact with high-structured bones that were seemingly still flowing with the warmth of her blood. I felt my own cheeks flush with the rush of my own blood. The beauty that blanketed her face made me catch my breath. She wore an enchanting shimmering Phoenix-red dress and pearl-like cashmere white stockings and around her neck hung a buttery-gold strand of black and white pearls. The angelic woman, clutching a crystal lilac orchid in her hands, looked like a tall, black Ethiopian Queen asleep in a sheath of light. The Negro woman's face held an ethereal, sublime, and timeless beauty that made me want to become like her. Still, sleeping she had an enduring presence.

"Sunshine Black?"

Ambrose nodded.

I covered my mouth and closed my eyes. The night's frost hit my burning cheeks. The aroma of the night garden swallowed me up. Her beauty made me cry. A tear slipped from my right eye.

"From divine beauty comes the essence of all things. Sunshine's heart was like the azure deep. Still, she is writing," he told me in a compassionate voice, never taking his eyes off me.

I chewed on the inside skin of my jaws with my back teeth until I felt the skin break and the taste of fresh blood warm my tongue like a mother's welcomed milk.

"Only Azrael could give Sunshine what her earthly life denied her."

I wanted to scream, but I didn't. Instead, I focused my eyes on some wormwood. An owl flew over our heads and landed into young birches that were casting a veil of transparent purple into the night garden with their heathery limbs.

Ambrose turned his back to me and walked over to the mouth of Peace Stream and looked into the three tall white young birches and mumbled, "Ashes of rose — just as the juniper becomes sweetest when flung into the flame, so did Sunshine Black."

I nodded and bowed my head and offered up a prayer to God to remove a sorrow I could not describe from my heart. When I opened my eyes, I saw an opening in the trees shaped like an emerald-arched window. That window framed an old mystery tree that looked like a tall witch weaving a spell against the wind in front of a luminous fountain draped with eternally sleeping blue roses. While imagining what Ambrose Twain had done to Sunshine Black in the name of love or vice versa, for the first time in my life, I screamed into the blank of my mind.

Ambrose said into the dark, "Sunshine was the only woman who could slay me with a glance. Though we were once slaves, we used to dream of Judean double rainbows trimmed in gold over the waters of the Island of Dawn."

The wind blew into the night garden in sudden, moaning gusts. Then it disappeared like vapor. When an owl laughed, I felt my eyes go round.

"There is an eternal strain between the soul and the poisonous memories that soak it with yesterday's rain. Only in an everlasting sleep called Death do you feel what a waking life has denied you," he told me then added, "*Listen.*"

"Listen for what?"

"Sometimes we listen to the sounds of silence; at other times we listen to the voices of others—all learning comes from something other than ourselves."

I looked over to some old junipers and noticed a ladder that had a hammer alongside a pair of rusty pincers that were lying on its third step. My thoughts made me shake worse than the wind. I looked down and saw white and green Georgia-marble steps tinged with ivy and Dead Man's Fingers that led to Peace Stream. I began to count the marble steps—thirty-three—trying to separate a portion in the waters of my mind from the lifeless feeling that was trying to ambush me.

Then like an angel ascending the staircase in Jacob's dream, Ambrose began to climb the steps toward the stream while weeping.

Instinctively, I followed him.

Once at the mouth of the water, he stopped climbing. "Ashes of rose, Sunshine is always listening—sleeping—to the sounds of silence. And I wait."

"Wait for what?"

"Someone to write her words for me. I wanted to give her the morning star, but I could not."

My voice now growing thin and low, "*Excuse me?*"

He bent down, reached into a little hollow hole in the earth and brought forth a silver-plated memory book that was inlaid with a bronze hawthorn. Gently, he placed the memory book in my hands. I opened it and began to read aloud this entry,

"1727, 19 January

My name is Sunshine Black. When I left New Orleans to go to New York to write about the lowly and the highborn, my folks said I was heady indeed. And they were right."

Ambrose Twain looked at me and asked, "Why did you leave the South and move to New York?"

"Excuse me?" I asked him.

When he looked away, I read on,

"It was Ambrose Twain who led me away screaming from the casket that had held the mortal remains of my Créole daddy, Jeremiah Raphael Black. Jeremiah was a good-looking man. What killed him were his weaknesses — moonshine whiskey and wild women. Alice Faye Bryant, his girlfriend, shot him right between the eyes over a bottle of Strip Go Naked Gin at Madame Fleur's Voodoo Parlour. Jeremiah left behind two things: a deck of Tarot cards and his only valuable possession, a

beloved 15th Century Spanish Civil War — as it was told me — Matchlock
Pistol. He willed both to me."

When Ambrose attempted to engage me in conversation with,
"Sunshine, *you wrote to me* about the lowly and the highborn." I
decided the best thing I could do was to let him have a conversation
with himself.

"Amid the French Quarter — Place d'Armes — with Jeremiah's war
pistol in hand, I took my last walk down the steps of St. Louis Cathedral,
on the arm of Ambrose Twain once the casket was closed. A white-white
butterfly breezed by us when we walked past Andrew Jackson's statue
then on to St. Peter's Street. Jeremiah Raphael Black was laid to rest
beside his beloved, Polly Sophia Black, in a little then private cemetery
belonging to the Holy Mother Mary Church in New Orleans."

"You wrote to me," Ambrose echoed himself.

I stopped reading.

Ambrose turned and gave me a long look that reminded me that I
used to write every day in Merrihope. My remembering pain was still
great.

*"After the St. Peter's Street cemetery, Ambrose and I walked along the banks of the Mississippi River. The Louisiana air was humid and salty even in January. Without warning, the word **Death** dropped into the blank of my mind. That was when I said, 'Let's take a ride on the St. Charles Line.' We took the 951."*

Ambrose asked, "Why don't you visit your family more?"

"My family burned up in the Merrihope house fire — my house — the one I once lived with my folks in until I moved to Goodlife, that is," I told him.

Silence.

"The air hit my face. I closed my eyes and let the smell of the Mississippi River and New Orleans fill me with odors I'd long forgotten. Crying, I said, Jeremiah wore blue roses in his eyes for most of my life. He could not be found on the day I was born. The only thing he ever bought me was a travel guide to New York that caught fire from me trying to read it by candlelight once he'd emptied his Strip Go Naked Gin bottle into his fat belly. On Friday nights, he would make his way through the French Quarter until he found the best boiled shrimp with new potatoes and freezing cold street beer to bring home to Momma and to me — their Sunshine. After we ate, he'd pretend to sleep and then

sneak out the back door. Years filled with Momma's weeping and his cursing passed. We filled our nights with ironing until daylight and dreaming of me going to New York to become a writer so I could rescue Momma and me from lives filled with nothing but loneliness. We had no friends. We didn't dare let anyone into our nothingness for fear of being found out that we were Nobody's from New Orleans. And worst of all, we had no love—shared or otherwise."

I stopped reading until Ambrose moaned and motioned for me to continue.

"Remembering back to the 951, Ambrose slipped a stand of black and white pearls around my neck and said, "Sunshine, move back South—I will try to love you."

Ambrose smiled to himself, bent over and laid on top of the glass coffin positioning himself directly on top of Sunshine Black. Then, through the glass, he began to trace the black and white pearls as if each one held a letter that needed to be strung into words to tell their story of love from a world that no longer existed or that perhaps, never even was save for in his imagination.

Sunshine wrote,

"*Sheets of silver rain began to fall. The St. Charles Line stopped, and when we got off, the world as we knew it to be in 1727 disappeared behind a silver screen of rain. Once on the other side, we found shelter beneath a moss-draped oak tree. I wrote Death.*"

DEATH

"*When the sun's eclipse enters the hidden heart of man, there is neither day nor night, only silver sheets of rain that gently entrance the mind's bluest eye without warning to its musical spheres.*"

"*Like a gift thrown down by God to me, Ambrose Train entered my life on a blue and white cloud floating amid a fainting sky decorated with early sapphire stars disguised by nature as a man. We became one. He was my first mistake—my original sin. My second mistake was keeping Jeremiah's pistol underneath my pillow.*"

"*Oh, night wind, lover of azure and fragrant with delicate sandalwood, why do you let eternal tears fall from your eyes only to leave my soul empty?*"

"*Two jewel-seekers are we dreaming double rainbows trimmed in gold over the mind's*

Horizon already pink with morning never to shine as One in Aeaea."

"The next day I returned to New York. My letters never stopped to Ambrose Twain until I moved and Jeremiah's pistol disappeared."

I stopped reading, closed the memory book, searched my mind for words, but none came.

Ambrose broke the silence. "Ashes of rose, will you set Sunshine's soul free?'

I swallowed hard and said, "All I know to do is put out the flame."

Ambrose's eyes filled with grace and passion. He nodded and smiled.

I bent then stuck my right hand in the midnight water of Peace Stream. The water was warm. As I took my hand out, I caught a glimpse of a pair of fish swimming keenly amid the dark, flowing waters of its purling water.

Ambrose reached into the stream and brought back a sparkling flower and said, "Ashes of rose, my gift to you—a diamond gardenia."

The night wind blew in a woodsy smell.

I took the sparkling flower and examined it with the eyes of a child. It was glorious. I opened the memory book, placed the diamond gardenia in its center like a bookmark before I handed it to Ambrose. With Ambrose watching, I walked the thirty-three steps back to where

Sunshine Black's beautiful black body lay suspended in Time. I saw a lotus flower growing in the mud beside her grave light. I took a deep breath and cast my own feelings aside for a stranger's soul as I stomped on the ice-blue light until I felt beauty join energy. I reached for some juniper to further smother the grave light. The shrubs produced faint glints of gold. A black and purple vapor filled the night air. I was surrounded by glints of gold dust. I felt something enter the blank of my mind and begin writing on the table of my heart. I couldn't read the words. I knew there were many. I knew that my memory would keep them safe like Ambrose had Sunshine's and his—even in Death—until it was time to call them up again. Feeling like a cracked soul, I whispered, "Forgive me."

My cheeks burned as if scorched by the fumes of darkness. An owl flew over my head into the arms of the older dark skinned trees and then straight at the candlelit tops of the three tall young, white skinned birches.

A lark let out a cry.

I looked and Ambrose had his ears cupped with his hands.

I ascended the steps and joined him at the mouth of Peace Stream. He turned and handed me the silver memory book, and the bronze hawthorn fell from its cover into the midnight, warm waters of Peace

Stream. I took the diamond gardenia out and offered it back to him. He took it and flung it into the zenith of the stream.

I waited.

Ambrose began to dance and dance and dance, bursting the fragrant juniper dark with nothing more than his own music of pure cold silence. Instinctively, I joined him. We danced like a muse and a maiden through the night garden beneath the full moon to the sound of silence, entering the Quick of Time until we became one in spirit.

Ambrose Twain vanished from Goshen, and I returned to Magnolia Sunday to write.

THE DEVIL'S WIFE

Clarity

"I am the Devil's wife," she began her story one spring Sunday afternoon in Goodlife to Johnny Paul Russell, Margie Anne Roberts, and me, Myra Boone. "It was long ago—you see—before I could become a gleam in anyone's eye that I woke up in a burning bed."

We listened.

She was black. And she was white. She was slim. Tall in stature. Her eyes penetrating with such palatable intensity that the color they once were, or might still be, was no longer totally visible to the naked eye.

Looking around the parlor, "I was color-blind. My hearing became impaired, but I wasn't deaf when I fell ears-over-head in love with the Devil. He first took me to the Land of 10,000 Dances," she told us with a broken smile.

Margie Anne's eyes widened.

Johnny Paul Russell shook his head from side to side like a bobblehead doll then cried out, "You wuz smitten like love with a kitten!"

"I hated my life then. And I hate my life now. Like many women before me and like me now, I couldn't distinguish between the voices of good and evil. Make no mistake—the Devil wasn't my first source of temptation. I had no connection to divine wisdom. I had no power to channel the necessary energy to resist. I guess you could say that it was by my own choosing that I fell *hard and quick* for the dances," she said with earnest.

"What kind of dances?" I asked.

"Word dances. *Beau-ti-ful* word dances," she replied, paused, took a deep breath, released it and then added, "One, ten, one hundred, one thousand then ten thousand all a-flame in a burning bed!"

We three simultaneously darted our eyes until a supportive connection was made and felt between us. I wasn't frightened of her.

She was more than familiar. Though unspoken to confirm, I sensed I had known her before I had even known myself. It was as if she was a part of the whole of every woman that I had ever known in my life of going on thirteen years. Too, she reminded me of myself only much older. It wasn't the questionable color of her skin either. It was something that I faintly saw in the center of her eyes. When I was able to get a glimpse into the center of her eyes, I saw a tiny diamond-shaped mirror that held an initial. When I looked deeper into both her eyes, I clearly saw an L in each eye. The more I looked into her eyes, I found that I wanted to reach in and take out each L and place each one upright on a shelf like two bookends — a pair of bookends that would support her own word dances to we three.

"Like I said — I hate my life," she told us then asked, "Do you like fruit?"

"Yes," we answered in unison.

She reached behind her onto a shelf and brought back a gold bowl filled with scarlet pomegranates.

Johnny Paul jumped up and dug into the front left side pocket of his navy blue overalls and brought back a double-blade black jackknife. He placed the pomegranate in the middle of an old shoebox lid with its crown side up. He soon opened then began to deseed it with his double-blade jackknife. He placed his white handkerchief aside on her Depression glass top fancy coffee table for later.

She reached beneath her chair and brought back a stack of brightly polished sterling silver saucers and gently placed them beside the gold bowl on top of her Depression glass top fancy coffee table. There were two bronze bowls on the fancy coffee table too. One was trimmed in silver, and another trimmed in gold. The one trimmed in silver held one blue rose while the one trimmed in gold held six blue roses. Accompanying the blue roses were feathery thorned asparagus ferns. There was a black and white book that divided the two bowls of blue roses. At first, I was unable to read the name on its worn, wrinkled spine. I squinted my eyes until I made out its title—"Good Hearts, Evil Hearts."

Margie Anne shrugged then went for the sterling silver saucers.

"It's not always about how a body treats you—it's about how a body *doesn't* treat you. And that's what breaks your very existence—mainly your will to live." She stopped talking and looked around the room before setting her eyes on we three and asked, "Do you know how to kill a body while she or he is still alive?"

We shook our heads no.

"Silence," was her one word answer.

We nodded.

"I am speaking to you three as a knowing soul. I've been dead—spiritually that is—for many, many years. I've been too ashamed to lift up my face to heaven and pray. I've cried for much of my life even before I married the Devil."

"Do tell. Well, I can tell you from experience that when you are ready to lift up your face and talk to your Heavenly Father, He'll be right there waiting to listen," Margie Anne said while Johnny Paul continued to deseed a pomegranate for each of us with his double-blade jackknife. They looked like red juicy diamonds sparkling amid the sterling silver saucers.

"*You think*?" she asked Margie Anne.

"Oh, yes! I'm sure of it," Margie Anne confirmed.

She went into deep thought and seemingly took note of Margie Anne's words then told us, "There is another way to *slowly* shut down a body too..."

We waited.

"Loneliness. Believe me, loneliness kills. Loneliness is ageless too."

I was the first to speak up, "I believe you. Sometimes even though I'm know I'm alive; I feel dead—inside that is," I told her.

"Girly Girl, me too!" Johnny Paul shouted then added, "If you wuz to cut me right now with my own double-blade jackknife, I wouldn't even bleed a drop of blood. I know I wouldn't.   My Paw is the same way. The only difference between us is our ages. Me and Paw, that is."

Margie Anne looked at us then around the parlor but didn't say a word. She pushed her thick glasses back up onto her nose before she adjusted her signature chiffon neck scarf. She was never without one. She wore it to hide the bruises made by her momma when she lost her temper—every other day or so—on her. Everyone knew that Margie Anne's momma hated her guts. No one knew why though, only that she did. Her chiffon neck scarf was most always tied in a bow. It not only hid her black and blue spots; it made her look like a pretty present no matter what color it was. She was sporting a pink one.

Funny, how folks can find ways to hide or cover up what's going on in their lives.

Up until I had moved to Goodlife, I had always thought I was the only one that was hiding what was *really* going on—inside and outside—of me. I gave Johnny Paul a half-smile. I knew it didn't matter if he was a little right or a lot wrong or both. All that mattered was that he, like me, believed what he said and felt what he felt... That was our truths—thoughts and feelings. Right or wrong. Good or bad. Our thoughts and our feelings were all we had—all either one of us had—to take us to visit our neighbors. What others thought of or believed or even said about us—dead or alive—didn't matter at all. And never would. That much I knew to be true about Johnny Paul and me.

It was the Devil's wife who spoke next, "When Jesual was proclaimed the Son by the Father, my husband became jealous. He believed he was the brighter of the morning stars. And that jealousy gave birth to sin and then Death. Let me tell you three, things in the underworld, or in any world for that matter, aren't always what *others* believe them to be. I'm living proof of that."

Margie Anne interrupted, "What *others*?"

"The *religious* spirits. That's who. And I can't assure you that they will ever listen because they have *never* listened. Religious spirits condemn. Let me be the first to inform you: The religious spirits that exist today and those of ages passed will never fully listen."

Looking up from a pomegranate, Johnny Paul asked her, "Are you a witch?"

I shrugged at Margie Anne. To me, she didn't seem evil like a witch was said to be at all. Just the opposite — she seemed pure. Angel-like even. *Unless* she had *another* side to her... But I didn't know *that much* about witches either though I did know that often people have more than one side to them.

She laughed like a hyena then cried out, "Men of all ages always *think* women are witches when they can't figure them out!"

Strangely enough Johnny Paul didn't challenge her with words or with his usual inquisitive, borderline argumentative Russell reply. Instead, he asked, "Won't you tell us more about the Devil?" He reached and took his white handkerchief from her Depression glass top fancy coffee table, cleaned his fingers and his hands, leaving it stained with the red juice of the now fully deseeded pomegranates. Then, he folded it in the shape of a diamond, and with great care he stuffed it halfway into his back pocket, somehow managing to hide the red stains.

She put on a favorable face and gave us an upward blissful smile that quickly turned to a defeated, sorrowful check. The left side of her upper lip got stuck. Her mouth began to quiver; then her face became yellow. Her angel-like appearance faded away, Suddenly, she looked more human and much older, now showing us her *other* side. But she didn't let anything stop her from talking on. I don't even think she knew or perhaps cared what her appearance was — at least not anymore or like she probably once had. *As if* she even had *any control*, I suppose, of how she looked from one minute to the next, beings *she was* the Devil's wife.

"Long ago, or maybe even yesterday, there was a knock at the door of my heart. When I opened it, I saw a person of great size and tallness. I asked, 'Who are you?' And he replied, 'I am your beloved.'"

It was Margie Anne who asked, "You mean to tell us that you *really* didn't know it was the Devil?"

She shook her head no. Her face broke in half from her forehead to her chin making her pain clear to me.

Johnny Paul gave me an inquisitive look but didn't speak.

"Do you *think* I would have let HIM in?" she asked us then said, "I didn't feel *anything* in my soul when I first met my husband. It was the week before Easter and Resurrection Sunday... I should have known by my own emptiness. Maybe I did. Maybe I didn't. Still, I'm not sure how it happened *to me*. How I fell *in love*, that is."

"Did he have horns? A tail? Was his face red? Did he spit fire? Did he have a pitchfork or a snake in his hands? Could he fry a T-bone steak between his teeth or on his head? What did he look like?" Johnny Paul asked her.

Without hesitation, "No, no, no, no, no, no, no, and no. The Devil looks just like you and every other soul you and I both know. Contrary to the pictures you see in the holy books, the Devil isn't ugly, scary, or even unpleasant to look at. How could a bright morning star be something that you couldn't stand to look at?"

"Well, Girly Girl, just how do you like *that*?" Johnny Paul asked me. He stood up straighter, and with his shoulders held back, he gave me an important look.

I smiled at him.

"You three must know that in the beginning, my husband and Jesual sang together in the constellations until jealously entered one of their hearts."

"How did the Devil enter *your* heart?" Margie Anne was quick to ask.

"You mean, how did he take me off the path to purity?"

"Yes, I suppose so," Margie Anne replied, face now flushed. She pushed her thick glasses back up onto her nose and tapped her pink bow once.

Johnny Paul spoke up and asked, "Did he give you whiskey?"

"Not a drop!"

"How then?" he asked her.

"I will tell you three how I became the Devil's wife. Keep in mind that what I am about to tell you is contrary and will break the ideas and images that you have of good and evil. Fair enough?"

"Fair enough," we three said not in unison but bouncy like the notes E, G, B... like three lines on the treble clef.

"Kindness. People don't think the Devil can be kind. They wrong. Yes. They wrong. The Devil can be anything and everything a body wants in order to penetrate the heart of the one he's set his eyes on. Truth be told, I blame my grandma that I married the Devil," she confessed.

"*Your Grandma?!*" I shouted, knowing mine was raising me.

"Yes. After she'd passed on, it was told me by my mother that she said the first question a woman should ask herself to consider before marrying a man was, 'Is he good and kind?' Little did I know that the Prince of Shadows, the enemy of humanity would take on human form and walk right in and sit down on the table of my heart with his kindness. *Loving kindness* such as it was—such as it is—today. He, too, was good. Good means next to nothing when it comes right down to it. By it, I mean, l-o-v-e. Yes, my grandma's advice had *consequences.*

All advice from others has consequences. I should have listened to *my* heart and thought with *my* mind. You three, always, always, always listen to your own heart. And mind. Learn early on to listen to yourself. Forget going to others for help. Be independent. *Only* depend on yourself."

We listened until a wide-eyed Johnny Paul interrupted our thoughts with, "Does that make you a princess?"

"Funny, you should ask. Day one, my husband—the Devil—made me *feel* like a princess all right."

"I bet he did!" Margie Anne cried out.

She nodded. "Is the pomegranate an o-k-a-y fruit for you three or not?"

We nodded. We had yet to take a bite of her food offerings to us though.

She reached over into a little basket beside her and brought back three gold spoons. She motioned for Johnny Paul to take them. He obliged her and placed a spoon on each of our sterling silver saucers. She declared, "Silver and gold I share with you while you are here in the Devil's house with me."

Simultaneously, we bent our bodies then necks forward and eyed the pretty serving pieces and red juicy jewels, but still, we didn't taste them.

Johnny Paul asked her, "Would you tell us *exactly* what the Devil looks like?"

Without hesitation, "When he can look much like you and me, except the Devil's eyes often turn as black as a raven especially when he's angry. He can be anything he wants to be to gain your trust. No one ever knows it's him. I tell you no lie. He can, he *will*, inhale your soul. You don't feel it. When he exhales it into the part of hell he fancies for you, it is *then* that you know you've been fooled by thinking you are *beloved* by him. Never ever believe a word that comes out of his mouth. The Devil only loves himself."

I looked to see if she was fighting back any tears. Her eyes were dry.

"And the Devil's love is conditional. He gives you a gift *only* to get something back from you. It's usually something you never intended to give to anyone. Something you've saved for yourself though you will come to forget who you are. Even what your real name is. Sometimes, my husband changes my name to a name he wants me to have. That makes me his. To others, I am "his wife." I had to become someone else just to survive living with the Devil. I am ashamed of that. You three are the only ones in Goodlife that knows I'm married to the Devil."

As we listened on, I knew she as telling us the truth—her truth—anyway.

"The Devil kept track of what he did for me. He wrote it all down in a memory book. He keeps good records too. He never forgets what he's given to or bought for me or anyone else for that matter. When I tried to repay him, it took me years *and then some* to learn that I could never repay a debt, any debt that I found myself owing my own husband. I know I can never repay the Devil one red-cent. Yes, I know because year after year, I became a prisoner by my own device. I've never been able to leave. I blame myself most of all. If you want to know the truth about it, I don't blame my grandma or anyone else anymore. I used to blame others until I grew up—until I grew old—until I told myself the truth—until I took responsibility for my own actions."

"Have you been to hell? Where is it?" Johnny Paul asked her then added, "My Paw is always tellin' folks to go to hell. And they git mad and stomp off, cursin' him and us. They always curse me and Maw. Like whatever he said or done wrong is our fault too. I hate that!

Neither me nor Maw had one cottin' pickin' thing to do with whatever they is mad at my paw about either! Yep, we always get blamed for his whiskey-talk."

To my surprise, Margie Anne didn't speak up to correct Johnny Paul's English like she usually did. I was glad of that. I knew it must embarrass him because as long as I had known him, he'd never spoken so much as one complete sentence with words that even resembled perfect English. And he probably never would.

"Yes. Right here — in Goodlife — where else would, *could*, hell be?

Johnny Paul shrugged.

Margie Anne gave her a hard look but didn't speak.

The Devil's wife stood and walked into another room and came back with a cardboard box. She took something out and placed it on the Depression glass top fancy coffee table.

We watched her close.

She said, "This is what the Devil gave me for a wedding gift."

We three bent forward to see bones of some sort in a cardboard box.

It was Johnny Paul who asked, "What is *that*?"

"Hand bones," she replied.

"What are they *for*?" Johnny Paul asked her.

"The Devil told me they belonged to one of his other wives," was her explanation.

Margie Anne cried out, "Mercy!"

It's no wonder she's never left him. My hands may have scars on them from the Merrihope house fire that killed my folks, but at least I still have them.

"My husband told me that he once lived in Rome. Being childless, *so it has been told of me*, the Devil warned me about what the *religious* spirits can do and *will do* to babies birthed by sinful *and marked* women like me."

Johnny Paul spoke up and asked her, "Are you talkin' about Rome, Mississippi? That's right near where my paw's brother is livin'—in Parchman—the Mississippi State Penitentiary. Right slap dab in the middle of the Mississippi Delta, I reckon you could say. Yep, he's got a few more Christmases to spend in the pen 'fore they let him out to come back home for Christmas dinner with his family unless someone can scrape together enough money to hire him a lawyer from Jackson to get his behind outta the pen."

Margie Anne sat a hard look on Johnny Paul, but he didn't even notice.

The Devil's wife turned and looked at Johnny Paul but didn't answer his question.

"If you'd like to visit the underground cellar in my house, I will oblige. I can show you, my babies." She stopped speaking, looked around as if she was looking for someone else other than we three in the parlor. "I'm not sure when my husband will be home. I don't want him to catch you three here, let alone me, in the underground cellar. He'll never forgive me for having company! Why there's no tellin' what he might do if he comes home and finds you three here."

I knew that she was telling the truth. And because of that, I was afraid for her. And us.

It was Johnny Paul who spoke, "Now, we wouldn't want to get you in trouble with your husband especially if he's the Devil."

I heard Margie Anne swallow hard.

"I believe that sometimes I see the babies open their eyes when I enter the underground cellar." She stopped speaking and set her eyes on Margie Anne and me before saying while exercising her Jupiter finger, "Carmelite sisters."

We three looked at each other and shrugged.

The Devil's wife turned, set her eyes on me, and waited.

Johnny Paul turned and looked directly at me too.

I decided to speak up, "I'd like to see your babies," while I had the courage.

Margie Anne gasped.

Johnny Paul cried out, "Girly Girl, what do you mean by asking to go into an underground cellar? Why, I bet you a shiny new penny that it's pitch dark down there! Well, we might as well go see a'fore her husband gets home. Ain't got nothin' else to do on a Sunday afternoon but go and see our neighbors anyway."

"Come, I'll show you three some of my secrets that happened through the passing of time."

"How can they be secrets if *you* know about them?" Johnny Paul asked her.

"Come with me," she instructed us. "You three can see what I'm taking about for yourselves."

After we exchanged glances, we stood and got in a single line to follow her through the living room into the kitchen where she opened a door to the right of a tall free-standing beveled glass mirror.

"Why you got a pretty mirror like that in your kitchen?" Johnny Paul asked her.

She blared out, "Where I won't fall asleep!"

"*Cooking?*" Margie Anne asked her.

"Living with the Devil you learn to be careful about every single thing. He can have one of his "smashing spells" if he even senses the food, or anything else for that matter, isn't p-e-r-f-e-c-t. You can never relax when you cook his breakfast, dinner, or supper. I am always walking on the tips of my toes. I can never burn anything. I've done so on more than one occasion, but I ended up with bits of glass in me from the smashing. Even if I part my hair on the wrong side—not in the middle, my husband gets angry with me. The Devil can *and will* destroy your feelings—your good feelings—with his word dances if you aren't careful—if you aren't to his liking—p-e-r-f-e-c-t."

"Are you good at tippy toeing?" Johnny Paul asked her.

"I've gotten good at it. I'd had years of practice. Yes, I can get through my day or my *present* circumstances without..." Her words trailed off leaving something like an unfinished thought in the air or maybe even a memory or two or even three.

Margie Anne cried out, "The Devil sounds like my momma! She's always losing her temper with me. Or *on me!*" She pushed her thick glasses back up onto her nose then adjusted the bow on her pink chiffon scarf.

Johnny Paul offered, "Maybe they is kin? Don't cha know that everybody in the South is somehow or another related? Hell, if I ain't careful, I could end up marrying my cousin or some other family member!"

"Could be..." she pondered.

Johnny Paul volunteered his help, "Wait—do you wear short shorts? Paw has one of them smashing spells like you're talkin' about when he comes home from jan-i-tor-ing at the bank and my maw has on short shorts, or even worse, a bathing suit. He gets fiery mad and breaks up plates, cups, and saucers if he comes home for dinner and catches Maw outside in the sunshine half-naked in her short shorts or her one-piece orange bathing suit." Margie Anne frowned at Johnny Paul when he cried out, "Maw says that somebody needs to put a hammer right between his eyes! I told her, 'Well, it ain't gonna be me. Maybe when the twins—Judy and Jerry—grows up, one of them can take Paw on with a hammer but not me!'" He paused to catch his breath then asked her again, "Tell me, do you wear short shorts or not?"

The Devil's wife did not answer Johnny Paul's question; instead, she said, "You three, come and see the babies... I will show you before my husband comes home for supper. I got it ready on the stove top. He'll never know I showed you. He *thinks* he knows everything that goes on in this house *and* in Goodlife, but he doesn't know *as much* as he *thinks* he knows."

I watched her close to see if I detected any untruths in her words.

"I am feeling stronger than I usually do. Having talked to you three today must have helped my feelings. I never talk to anyone. Not even my family. After I married the Devil, I gave up my friends. I gave up what family I had too. He *marked* me with his number. I'm his and his alone." She stopped speaking, bent over, pushed the hair off the nape of her neck, and in the small of her head, about an inch or so into her hairline, was a smoky, black-inked tattoo of the number 616. She resumed to her upright standing position and continued on with, "You three must promise me that you won't ever tell a soul. Not even in a winter blizzard if you find yourself cold and afraid and wanting to keep warm by huddling together and telling stories to say awake..." She stopped speaking for a few seconds then said, "Raise your right hands and say, 'I solemnly swear before God Almighty I won't tell what I am about to hear *and see* here today in this underground cellar in my house.'"

Johnny Paul spoke up first, "I'm left-handed."

"Me too," Margie Anne told her.

The Devil's wife set her eyes on me and asked, "Are you left-handed too?"

"I am," I told her.

She cried out, "Well, left-hand swears don't count! Not in my book anyway. I guess I am either going to have to trust you three, or I'm not."

We waited for what seemed like an eternity for her to decide if she would place her trust in us.

Johnny Paul turned and gave her two thumbs up.

Margie Anne pushed her thick glasses back up onto her nose then adjusted the bow on her pink chiffon scarf and gave her a sweet smile.

I stood up straighter, shifted from heel to toe then toe to heel with both feet simultaneously before I crossed my fingers under my left arm for luck.

Then without any further hesitation, she beckoned we three with her Juniper finger to follow her down steps into a dark, cold, and damp underground cellar. Before taking another step down, Margie Anne stopped and made the sacred sign of the cross in midair. Then she said, "Protect us, Sweet Jesus," evoking God's protection on us.

There was a holy hush that soon followed. Caught up in the mystery of the moment, neither had entered my mind to do. Even if it had, I don't know that I would have done so anyway. Much of the time, my hands were too sore and too tired to hold a fork, let alone make a cross in midair. And on some days, my legs felt too weak and bruised from the inside out to hold me up most of the day long. Since the Merrihope fire that took away the only three people I'd ever loved in this world—Momma, Daddy, and Great Aunt Annabelle, I found that at the beginning or even the end of most days, I just existed and seemingly my spirit floated through Goodlife. I knew that *just existing* wasn't living at all. I did feel a measure of happiness living there and not having to copy entire books from the Bible like Momma had me doing for years in Merrihope to pass the time off. The scars on my hands always hurt me even though scars aren't supposed to hurt, mine did. I gave as much of myself away to my friends and my animals as I knew how to give, but still, I was always sad. Deeply sad. I didn't know *why* I had lived and *why* my folks had died. I felt bad about that. But like always, I never knew what to do or who to ask or what I should do to feel better. Even if I could feel a measure of relief from the guilt that I felt would surely follow me for the rest of my life, I would welcome that feeling of relief. I often thought that if I, too, had been burnt up in the house fire that I wouldn't be any worse off than being alive in Goodlife because sometimes my days were a living hell.

Every now and then, I felt as dead as the folks were in the cemetery. I didn't dare share this with my grandfolks. They were doing the best they knew how to make me happy. Although having people around helped me, I secretly hoped that there was more for me to do with the rest of my life than I was doing. There had to be some reason that I was left on earth and my folks were taken away from it. And me.

Is there really a reason for everything in life or is it that just something old folks tell young folks because they don't know the answers to their questions?

It was Johnny Paul who broke into my thoughts when he cried out, "Demons fly away!" He reached into his right pocket and brought back a bright, almost shiny, green lizard, gently blew on it until its neck puffed out, and turned rose-red like it had swallowed a new dime, then gently put it back into his pocket.

"Johnny Paul, what'd you do *that* for?" I asked him.

"My secret," was all he said then gave me a right-eye wink before adding, "For me to know and for you to find out. Girly Girl, I's got to keep some secrets for myself."

"Suit yourself then," was all I said.

Johnny Paul turned and asked her, "Wait—is the Devil black all over too like a crow?"

"Why would you ask me that?" was her reply.

"Because every time when Maw is washing our clothes in Taylor Creek, one of them black crows swoop down and steals her bar of lye soap off her washing board. Maw always hollers out, 'Them crows are full of the Devil! See how black they are? I don't care how much lye soap that Devil crow eats, it won't wash away his thevin'!'"

We three waited for her to answer him as if he'd hit on some characteristic, or maybe even a truth, of or about the Devil being black.

Again, she told him, "The Devil looks like you and every other soul you and I both know."

Margie Anne and I exchanged glances, and Johnny Paul gave a shrug.

Again, with her Juniper finger, she made a beckoning motion for the three of us to follow her. Being led by the Devil's wife, we three walked down many steps into a dark, cold, and damp underground cellar. She stopped walking and reached over and flipped on a light switch on a wooden beam that was midway down the stairs, and four lights lit up the four corners of the underground cellar. What we saw next sunk so deep into my veins that my blood screamed cold. I felt my blood freeze in my veins. I became sore afraid the death rattle was coming to me next. I was scared to a near death.

Along one wall of the underground cellar was a lacquered freestanding bookshelf made of wood. Instead of books on the shelf, there were shells of babies on it. I saw something that I can never unsee again. Corpses. Corpses of babies. Corpses of children. Corpses of both. At first, I thought there were going to be too many to count. But I was wrong. I think I was just dizzy. It was after I counted to myself that I realized that there were only six corpses.

"These babies are *my* babies. They belong to me," she told us.

After seeing what was on the bookshelf, Margie Anne looked stunned then shocked.

I asked, "What do you mean—*your* babies?"

"You three are the only ones I've ever let any further than the kitchen mirror into my life. After, I realized that I'd married the Devil, I became shamefaced. When he marked me with his number, I knew my life was no longer my own. Yes, I knew in our burning bed that I was a sinful woman and marked by the Devil. When I got *that way*, it occurred to me that I would have to keep my babies hid from the Devil and every other soul—dead or alive—in Goodlife."

Margie Anne cried out, "That's the worst thing I've ever heard in all my born days!"

"Are you a-tellin' us the truth? Or are you a-pullin' our legs?" Johnny Paul asked her.

"It be true," she told us with a broken blue face.

"Girly Girl, do you think we are going to get in trouble with her husband if he comes home and finds us in their underground cellar?" Johnny Paul asked me.

I shrugged.

"Let me finish what I started out to tell you three," she began and boldly approached the shells of the six corpses' where feathery thorned asparagus ferns were growing in and around them. The feathery thorned asparagus ferns softened the corpses. "Look, this was my first-born—David—a boy. Then, it was over the years that the rest came along—Nellie Pre Mellie who I named after my Maw. Maw went blind..."

Margie Anne butted in, "Listen, you don't have to tell us their names."

I asked, "Did you kill your babies?"

"Oh, no, one was born dead, and the others, well, they just died off over the years. I don't know why they died on me. After I brought my babies down into the underground cellar, one by one they eventually stopped crying. Only one was already dead when it shot out of my body like a cannon ball. I never tried to go and get help to see if they could be brought back to life though. I didn't try to get help when the others became sick and died off. I did cry though. No one ever came to see me anyway. Not a living soul. You three are the only ones I've seen in fifty or more years other than my husband."

"Why wouldn't you go get help?" Margie Anne asked her.

"L-o-v-e," she spelled then added, "I was afraid someone would take my babies from me. Dead or alive, I loved them. I didn't want to give them up. They are all I've ever had to keep me company. I even read to them and show them picture books and tell them Bible stories."

"That is the worst thing I've ever heard!" Margie Anne cried out.

"Why did you keep them?" I asked.

She replied, "Why not?"

"Can we see your babies up close?" Johnny Paul asked her.

With a new excitement, she nodded and motioned for us to come forward to see what was on the lacquered freestanding bookshelf.

We saw the shells of dead babies of various sizes. We saw young children, but none looked to be or had been older than five years old. There was no way to tell their ages. It was as if they were sleeping on the lacquered freestanding bookshelf. One baby was dressed in a long nightgown that looked to have once been a pretty pink color but had faded over the years, no doubt, into a rusty orange. It made me want to cry but I held my breath so I wouldn't. There was another baby with a little pair of faded navy-and-white-striped carpenter's overalls. Another one was wearing a white cotton dress like five pounds of biscuit baking powder came in at the Better Living Grocery Store in Soso. It looked as if it could have been a flour sack with three holes cut out—head and two arm holes. Twin corpses were wrapped in homemade quilts—one red, the other green. Like bookends, the twin corpses supported her explaining word dances to we three. I saw a baby swaddled in a raggedy corner of a faded canary-yellow bedspread. Feathery, thorned asparagus ferns blanketed, and from appearances alone, softened their eternal resting place on the lacquered freestanding bookshelf.

Margie Anne swallowed hard. She let out a sigh.

Johnny Paul cried out, "Oh, Lordy!"

I wasn't sure what to say or even if I should say anything at all, let alone if I needed to ask the Devil's wife any questions. In many ways, I was lost for words, but I wanted to say something to let her know that if she wanted to be like one of us again and let others into her life, that today was her chance. Because her head was down, I didn't know if she thought that she deserved anything good in Goodlife but her dead babies and the Devil for a husband. Neither of which, as far as I could see or tell, held anything good for her at all... anything good for anybody, ever, ever again.

"It was good of you not to forsake your babies," was all I managed to say.

With her head down, "You three please don't think less of me than I already think of myself. You see, I had no choice. I, too, had to protect my own flesh and blood from my husband. Listen, my aching soul told me that I had no choice. At least that's what I *truly thought* it was saying to me. I loved my babies enough to not let them live like I had been living with the Devil—not even for a day. I was afraid he'd mark them with a number like he'd marked me."

Margie Anne, Johnny Paul, nor I, said another word to her for what felt like fifty or more years of the life she'd had married to the Devil. As if we or anyone else would know what to say that would change one thing, she'd already done to herself and to her own flesh and blood—her babies or her children—such as they were, such as they ever were, if anything at all, were ever to have been. I knew right then and there that I didn't want to grow up and be like the Devil's wife, not even for a day let alone be without *any* company for fifty years of my life like she'd been.

"Why didn't you bury your babies?" Johnny Paul asked her.

"Believe me when I tell you that I saw no other way to have a family than to keep them all to myself. I kept them in the underground cellar. Always. All of their days. All of their nights. No one ever knowed until today. I guess I never wanted to let them go off and leave me alone. Dead or alive, I love them. That's all there is to it."

It was a teary-eyed Margie Anne who said, "I believe you."

Johnny Paul sniffled, nodded, and then said, "Me too. I might do the same if my dog, Butterbean, ever dies on me."

Margie Anne rolled her eyes then she gave Johnny Paul yet another hard look.

Before she turned to face us, I could hear her tears. And it was then that I felt sorrier for her than I'd ever felt for myself. I looked deeper into the underground cellar and asked, "What else is down here?"

"My pretties—my bottles," she replied.

"What kind of bottles?" Johnny Paul asked her.

She made a motion for us to follow her to another part of the underground cellar where we saw an entire wall of colorful glass bottles. I saw haint blue, lime green, bright—not dark sun-kissed—orange, light pink, rose-dawn, dawn-lilac, oystershell white, glittering gold, pure purple, canary yellow, berry red, and part gold and turquoise to name a few of the bottles that the Devil's wife had in her underground cellar.

"What's in them colorful bottles?" Johnny Paul asked her.

With a dreamy, sublime look in her eyes, "They is how I've stayed alive," she told us.

We three moved closer to the colorful glass bottles to see what was in them. All I could see was a clear liquid of some sort.

"Are they full of moonshine?" Johnny Paul asked her.

"No. Not even one bottle has moonshine in it. In the passing of time, I've saved all my tears. And right here on this bookshelf here be me tears for you three to see," she told us and reached for a haint blue glass large bottle that was shaped like a fish, uncorked it, and then held it up to her left eye and let the tears I was already hearing fall into the haint blue glass fish.

Margie Anne cried out, "*All* of them?!"

She confirmed, "All of them."

Johnny Paul was quick to ask her, "Where'd you git all these pretty glass bottles?"

The dreamy, sublime look in her eyes faded away. "From behind Shorty Stringer's place where mostly the White folks dump their garbage *and other* secrets along the Way can be seen. This goes on for hours well deep into the night amid the illuminations made by the People of the Way led by Veronica carrying her Veil and looking for the One with the cross," she answered him, recorked the fish bottle and gently placed it back onto the bookshelf.

"I thought you never go out. How'd you get them and know about the People of the Way and Veronica if you never go out?" Margie Anne asked her.

"I forgot that sometimes I do go out *only* after midnight when I wake up and see my husband ain't come home yet. I wander like a lonely wolf up and down the roads in Goodlife, and many a time I end up behind Shorty Stringer's place where the once slaves and Cordelia practice Hoodoo. By the light of the moon, I often take myself a glass bottle or two off an arm of one of their bottle trees that they create to draw the spirits—low and high—in."

Margie Anne raised her eyebrows at her, and then she cut her eyes at Johnny Paul who reached into his front pocket and took out his shiny bright green lizard and began to stroke it until it turned brown.

Again, he blew on it three times and gently placed it back into his pocket.

I saw that the Devil's wife was truly of a confused and lost nature. Yet, she seemed to be willing to let we three into her world, as dark and as painful a world that it was otherwise, we'd not be moving about ever so freely in her underground cellar. Though alive and breathing, she still had moments that felt lifeless, dead even, to me. Still, I wanted her to feel like one of us—the living—such as we were—again, not the blue rose that clearly, she now was or had long ago become. She seemed lost somewhere in between two worlds like me and many others in Goodlife and Goshen.

"What made you even think to do such a thing?" Margie Anne asked her.

"Sunday School," she replied.

We three asked in perfect unison, "Sunday School?"

"Yes," she confirmed.

"Why for?" Johnny Paul asked her.

"When I was a young girl, my Sunday School teacher, Shirley Stringer, gave me a Bible with a verse circled in red ink that made me a memory. I've held onto that memory for most of my life. See, my maw used to hit me over the head and anywhere else she could hit me with a black cast iron skillet to wake me up. By the time I got to Sunday School, I hurt all over and had the worst headache you can make yourself think of. Still, I have dents all in my head from that black cast iron skillet. After Paw left her with a house full of youngins', Maw was never the same. One day, she became as blind as a night bat. She used to bake birthday cakes for every one of us children and put up a Christmas tree. We'd even pop corn in the black cast iron skillet on an open fire then string it together to drape around the Christmas tree. Early one December morning after breakfast, Paw said that he was going out for a Coke-a-Cola and never come back home. Maw turned right mean after that."

We three watched her close, holding our breath for what was to come out of her mouth next.

"Believe it or not, I was a nervous child. Always a-feared of going off to sleep on account Maw might burn the house down with her tobacco smoking in the bed and I'd wake up dead. Mind you three, that fear had a strong hold on me and keep me bound to it for most, if not all, of my childhood years. That's why sometimes I can't sleep and walk many a mile deep within the dark of the night like a wolf. But Sister Shirley Stringer's voice somehow carried over into my days and my nights, of which, after the passing of time began to run together and became one and the same."

I heard Margie Anne swallow hard.

"Every Sunday morning, I was always crying. When Sister Shirley saw my tears, she took me aside and told me that my *loving* Heavenly Father kept track of *all my tears*. That He collects them in Heaven. Sister Shirley said that He keeps a written record of all our misery *and* of *all our tears*... That memory is what give me the notion to save my tears in a bottle. One Sunday morning Sister Shirley told me while reading the circled Bible verse—Psalm 56:8. It is written, 'Thou tellest my wanderings: put thou my tears into thy bottle: are *they* not in thy book?' It was over the years that I became more and more miserable and cried more and more. I always prayed I'd run out of tears, but I never did any more than I ran out of the air that I breathed in to form the words that I never could say to anyone until today. No one ever came my way until now. I figured that if my Heavenly Father had already been saving my tears in Heaven, then I would do the same, and that would make Him *proud* of me—doing the exact same thing as He was doing for me, I would do for Him. I reckon you could say it was my way of helping Him. I figured He was too busy with the highs, not the lows like me, and that He would run out of patience having to save my miseries and my tears... And that surely my *loving* Heavenly Father would see that *my saved tears* in these glass bottles are *my sacrifices* to Him beings Paw never came back home to see what or if I'd ever become anything other than a crying baby or child or woman or do anything good or bad with my life. Instead of collecting books to fill my bookshelf like most folks do, over the years I've collected many throwaway glass bottles from the garbage cans and the spiritual bottle trees to fill my bookshelf with my miseries and tears. My tears are my clarity. That's all I've done with my life—good or bad—such as it it—nothing more."

Margie Anne gave the Devil's wife a big smile before she said, "This is a beautiful bookless bookshelf—tears—and all. I love it. And the sacrifices you've made for your loving Heavenly Father make perfect sense to me."

Johnny Paul blared out, "Ain't enough glass bottles or beer cans to hold all the tears I've cried since the day I was born, that's for damn sure!" Margie Anne raised her eyebrows at Johnny Paul when he said, "Is your husband's people from up around the Delta? That's where the hoodoo folks come from. The reason I know is on account that Everett Bass asked my paw to help him run a truck of moonshine up their way once. And when Paw came back, he told me about that—

and when God began it all—Hoodoo that is. Paw told me that the Bible is the greatest hoodoo book there is. Paw said that he and Everett Bass took a Bible with them for protection up in the Mississippi Delta. Said they opened it up and sit it down slap dab in the middle of the road and waited."

Margie Anne interrupted with, "Waited for WHAT?!"

"Paw said without fail that the Bible will give anyone anywhere— saint and sinner the like—the direction they are seeking as they cross a road or walk straight up it. Paw said that hoodoo folks have know'd that all along and that they get a bad tongue lashing from the rest of the God-fearing, church going folks because of what they believe about the Lord God. My paw don't lie to me. He may do a lot of sorry and low-down things neither one of us is proud of, but he ain't never lied to me. That's much I know to be true. I can't count on Paw for much, but I can count on him to tell me the truth," Johnny Paul replied and gave us a proud look before adding, "Paw said, 'Son, you can lock up a thief, but you can't lock up a liar. Don't go to jail for a stupid lie!'"

Margie Anne noted, "Well, Hoodoo or not, I'm thankful my momma has never hit me with a black cast iron skillet. And the good

Lord knows that we have three of them nesting inside of each other. When I get back home, I may had better hide them from her."

Johnny Paul offered, "You give them to me, and I'll bury them for you right in the graveyard if you want me to. Or the next time Paw helps dig a grave over at the Union Cemetery, I'll throw them skillets into the hole before they put the body, I mean box, in. Just say the word, and I'll do it for you. Or I can throw them in the deep end of Taylor Creek, and nobody will ever find them again."

Margie Anne nodded at him.

"Are you a-feared of your husband?" Johnny Paul asked the Devil's wife.

Sure, and strong, "I threw all I knew of God—good or bad—to the wind when I married the Devil. Sometimes I hold my breath until I pass out, so I don't have to talk to him. Yes, I am afraid of him. And like I told you, I was too ashamed to pray. I became a fool." She stopped speaking for a moment then whispered, "But even fools have dreams."

"What do you dream about?" Margie Anne asked her.

"I will tell you three that last night I had a dream. And in my dream, I was dreaming of myself. I had been waiting a long time for someone to come along to talk to or for something new to occur in my life. I didn't know what I was waiting for, but I knew I'd been waiting or rather hanging in *the balance of time and judgement* for something to change in my life. In my dream, I saw a pearl of great price. At first, I thought it was a full moon but soon determined it was a pearl—yes, a gem of great price—a *perfect* gem of truth. Suddenly, the Devil appeared in my dream and offered out his hands to take the pearl from me. Without hesitation, I was about to hand it over to him. Then to much my surprise, I dropped it, and he disappeared forever like Paw did without ever saying another word to me."

"Where do you reckon the Devil went?" Johnny Paul asked her.

"Back from whence He came," she told us and faded away.

In silence, we three waited for her to reappear. And after a short while, when she did, she told us, "You three became as One and brought me my pearl today. By telling you the truth and sharing my secrets, I am no longer ashamed. I don't feel disgraced anymore." She paused, turned, and faced Margie Anne. "I want to lift up my face and pray beings you told me my Heavenly Father is right there waiting to listen..." She turned away from Margie Anne and exercised her Juniper finger at a large horizontal widow off to the side of the underground cellar while saying, "If you don't mind, please open that window and let yourselves out so that I can be alone with my babies and pray, not cry, in secret to my loving Heavenly Father."

It was Johnny Paul who spoke up and asked her, "What's your name anyway? How can we say goodbye without knowing your name?"

We waited.

"I, Lived," was her beautiful two-word dance to us.

And it was with clarity that I knew that the Devil's wife was living amongst us amid the rest of our neighbors in and around Goodlife.

LETTIE STRINGER

Joy

"Be independent," is what Maw always told me. "Learn how to take care of yourself. Don't depend on nobody on God's green earth to take care of you. Learn a trade," Lettie told me standing over an ironing board in her plain and simple kitchen ironing slow and careful and with great seriousness. Deliberate. Firm.

I nodded.

"That's why I learned ironing," she went on.

Looking around Lettie's kitchen, I saw an ice-box, a gas top stove, a kitchen table with three chairs, ill-matched dishes, a large jar of colored buttons, a small and a large pair of scissors, one place setting of plastic yellow and white daisy dishes, a set of stainless silverware for one, a clear plastic glass, an empty plastic garbage can of sorts, and a yellow kitchen wall clock with a timer that reminded me of an oversized pocket compass. There was a framed drawing of an open hand traced with a charcoal pencil near the light switch. Strangely enough, her kitchen cabinets were painted black. All in all, her kitchen was a neat as a pin.

Folks from Soso to Goodlife had told me *never* to go to visit Lettie — *ever*. Said she was an old, blind hermit Negro that had a *curse* on her. Something to do with alcohol. And love.

Nothin' right, let alone normal, about tha Negro Lettie! She be cursed! Why else would an old, blind woman be smiling with nothing to be happy about? She's crazy in the head, is what I had heard folks say.

With purpose, I had slipped off from Magnolia Sunday right after supper in the cool of the day and before dark to see a cursed old, blind hermit Negro woman for myself. I figured Lettie would at home being it told me that she only left her house to walk the roads after dark seemingly alone though folks said they always saw someone walking beside her holding her hand amid the early light.

"I make ends meet," she held up her iron and smiled before continuing with her work. "The good Lord splashed a dab of mercy on me and the fruit of my labor. I got a reason to live." Again, she held up her iron as if I were blind and not her.

She was wearing a peach-colored sleeveless shift dress with white dogwood blooms throughout. It had double-stacked deep pockets. A bright red-and-white bandana was neatly tied around her head. Round spectacles with jet-black lens shielded her eyes from my sight. And she was barefooted. Tall and skinny as a snake too. She was a pretty Negro—one of those ladies that it was hard to tell exactly how old she was. Cursed or not, I could see something deep within her that needed attention like an ageless child would.

As I was watching Lettie iron, she shook a button-down long sleeve shirt, placed it face down on the ironing board then pressed it out firmly with her hands first before she took one of two coal-black flat-irons from her gas top and began to press the shirt's backside in four sure and steady strokes. Then, she flipped the shirt over, buttons up, using her pointer fingers to press out its sleeve seams, and with two seemingly easy strokes, she ironed down the long sleeves on each side. She did the rest of the shirt with pretty much the same calculated, steady, firm moves, making ironing a button-down long sleeve shirt look effortless.

"Lettie, what happened to your eyes?"

"Myra Boone, I misbehaved. Two times in one day!"

Taken aback, I interrupted, *"Misbehaved? How?"*

"I failed to drop my eyes when my field boss man, Mister Styron, walked though one of the cotton rows I was picking from. He be a Whitey, you know? Being a Blackie, I knowed better than to look him directly in the eyes. I was taught early on like my maw before me and her maw before her to never to fail to drop my eyes when the boss man walks by," she said from behind her round jet-black spectacles—to hide her blindness, I suppose.

She waved at me. I waved back as if she could see. She was smiling. Her smile reminded me of folks saying she had a curse on her because they thought she had nothing to be happy about. Still, I was interested in what kind of a curse she may or may not have.

Pointing to the right side of her head with her Jupiter finger, "I was given a shot of rubbing alcohol right here in the temple. That be what caused my blindness," she told me.

I frowned. I felt sick to my stomach too.

Lettie was quick to ask me, "Myra Boone, you willing to learn?"

Nodding, "Yes, I'm more than willing to learn," I told her, forgetting she couldn't see me nodding.

Shouting, "Even from an old Blackie like me!"

"Once a real preacher man in Merrihope, Mississippi, said I had a *curse* on me because my folks had sinned or such."

She stopped ironing and smiled like a spider monkey before she told me, "Myra Boone, I can walk you down the only road I've ever been down since I lost my eyes for seeing."

Interrupting, "*What Road?*"

"Certainty Road," she said firmly.

"Lettie, how can we walk down the road together if you can't see?" I asked her, wondering.

With confidence, "Myra Boone, it's a straight road. That's how."

"Lettie, tell me, how do you live alone? Don't you have anybody to come around and see about you?"

"If you wuz not so young, I'd expect mayyy-beee you could understand —."

Feeling anxious, "Understand *what?*" I interrupted her before I knew it. I felt hurried around her like I was stealing her ironing time.

She waved at me before taking a deep breath, and after she pushed a few black and gray hairs from her forehead back under her bright bandana she said, "The boss man, Mister Styron, *fancied* me when I was spry and in my best years *until* he dropped by my first homeplace in the cool of the day after supper one evening and caught me laying down in my bed loving on my Chester. He fired me from working *all* the fields—cotton, peas, watermelon, and cantaloupe. He knowed straight off that he'd lost his bewitching power over me. He featured me *his* property. His thinking took to that of a ravenous wolf towards the rest of my family. He run them off on account of my unspoken love for my Chester. Nobody could pull me back into the fold—field or otherwise—of Mister Styron's workers, that is," she told me.

"*Why?*" I asked her.

"Said I was like chaff in the corn. So, he separated me. Took away my sight too. That way I couldn't ever see to love on anyone else again. I was never given a second chance for love—with anybody," she replied.

"Oh, no, Lettie! No!" was all I knew to say while I covered my own eyes.

"Oh, yes, Myra Boone, yes! After Mister Styron caught me loving on my Chester, he soon felt like the prong on a winnowing fork to me. Yes, he shook me in all ways. Thought he'd ruin my life," she went on before adding, "and took away my joy until I found it again." Lettie paused, looked up, and then said, "Myra Boone, I now got an obligation to help those that have the courage to come and see me—like you—find the same joy that I have found."

"*Really?*"

"I do."

"What happened to your Chester?"

"He was found floating face down in the freezing cold waters of Taylor Creek. They told me he drowned, but I knew it was a lie! A damn lie!"

"How'd you know it was a lie?"

"We went swimmin' every day that passed. That's how. And we washed up after the working in the fields. My Chester could swim like a fish, 'sides that! Yes, Myra Boone, he could swim, float, and knew how to trot the water, if you want to know the truth about it."

"Oh," was all I knew to say, knowing good and well I couldn't swim a lick. And was right embarrassed about it.

"Do you have any children?"

"I did."

"What do you mean *you did*?"

"Me and my Chester had the prettiest little sapphire blue eyed boy. He was eleven-year-old. Born on May 14 to my recollection. His name was Clay. He smiled all the time. We kept him hid though on account of his eyes. We'd never seen anything like them before in all our born days. Nobody had. Clay was right good-natured to be kept in the closet all the day long except when one of us would sneak back to the house to feed him and give him water and take him to the outhouse. Then right before I was given the shot of rubbing alcohol in my temple, a group of men showed up after supper one Sunday night, and they grabbed our Clay right out of my arms and took a hammer and, like a knocker does a pig, hit him hard, real hard, Myra Boone, right between his sapphire blue eyes!"

"Oh, Lettie, no!"

"Yes, they surely did! There was not one thang on God's green earth that me or my Chester could do to save him! He screamed and screamed and screamed until he bled out like a pig!"

"Do you know who they were?"

Lettie shook her head, no.

I felt my entire body tremble in fear.

"Know what else they did to my Chester?"

"What?"

"Cut both his ears off from his head. That's what!"

I gasped. "Why?"

"Dogged if I knowed. Just evilness that takes a-hold of some men in this world is all I know to tell you. Myra Boone, and that ain't all of it either! Then someone even more evil- minded than that put my Chester's ears in an envelope and walked deliberate-like up my front steps. I had steps at my first home place. That loud steppin' low manchild of Lucifer come and knocked on my screened door, and when I opened it, unbeknownst to me, I was handed the self-same envelope."

I interrupted, "Oh, no!"

"Oh, yes, I wuz! Being newly blind and trusting, I sat down in a chair, went on and opened it, and my Chester's ears fell out in my lap!"

"What did you do?"

"Screamed and screamed and screamed until I passed out."

I shivered. "Lettie, what did you do with your Chester's ears?"

"Said a prayer over them, and then I buried them out behind the house in a large-sized Diamond kitchen matches box I got from the gas top. I keep blue roses on the grave when I think about it."

Through gritted teeth, "That's right nice sounding, Lettie. How do you know they are blue roses?"

"That's mostly what grows in Goodlife. Do you want to know why they cut my Chester's ears off?"

"Not if you don't want to tell me, I don't. But if you want to tell me, I will listen," I told her. All the while she'd been talking to me, I was wondering how much sadness and pain a body could take and still smile.

"Sure, I want to tell you, Myra Boone. I got to tell somebody what's on my heart. I think, I dream, and I think more, and I dream more about my Chester's ears every time I lay my head down. And I see the blood flowing between Clay's sapphire blue eyes in my mind day and night. They wuz the two people this old Negro fool woman loved more than anything else in the whole wide world! That's why I stay awake more than most folks. I don't want any more remembering pain."

"Go on and tell me," I told her not wanting to be the cause of her remembering pain because I felt in my heart that she wanted to talk about her lost loved ones like me.

"Mister Styron told him to stay shed of me—only me! It was my Chester's punishment for not listening to the boss man. That's why!"

"Lettie, I am so sorry that happened to you and the two people you loved more than anything else in the whole wide world. My heart hurts for you…"

"Myra Boone, I thank you kindly for saying such to me. I cried every day for only the Lord God knows how long until I got a girlfriend, Maxine, in here to read to me from the Holy Bible. Reading give me comfort, especially when I learned by way of hearing what the Lord God says about joy and how His children were made to shine like stars. She read to me about this fellar named Job. His pain and suffering was just a test. The Lord God talked to him a lot. I love hearing about Job. Hearing his story makes me feel better, if you want to know the truth about it all."

"*Really?*"

"It do! Did you know that the Lord God knows each one of His children by name — before they were ever born?"

"No, Lettie. I don't think I've heard that before."

She smiled.

"The Lord God spoke to Job out of a whirlwind. He said to Job, 'Where were you when I laid the foundations of the earth? You, Job, sitting in your darkness. Get up and answer Me like a man! Do you understand what I'm talking about, Job?'"

"What did Job say to that?"

"As far as I know, he kept his mouth shut!"

I gave her a quizzical look. "What else did the Lord God say to Job?"

"He said, 'I demand that you get up and answer me! If you have *any understanding* at all, Job, get up out of your darkness and tell me, who laid the cornerstone of the foundations of this earth? And tell me, Job, who supports the earth's foundations and laid the cornerstone as the morning stars sang together and all the angels shouted for joy? Finally, the Lord God asked Job, 'Where is the path to the place where the light is divvied up?"

"Did Job get up out of the dark and answer the Lord God?"

"I ain't for sure. But I got up out of my darkness, and that's when I found my way to Certainty Road. Myra Boone, I found my own way."

"Lettie, when are *we* going to take that walk down Certainty Road?"

"Let me go pee first. Myra Boone, you got ta pee?"

"Maybe," I said thinking I'd better try to pee in case we were gone for a long time.

Lettie stopped her ironing. When she reached over to the gas top stove to set her iron down on an eye, that's when I saw a box of large Diamond kitchen matches.

I asked, "Lettie, did you ever try to love on anyone else again?"

Without hesitation, "Myra Boone, my Chester was my first love. Now he only exists in my heart. Don't you know that some people only exist in our hearts?"

"Yes, I know."

"That's one reason why I walk much of the night. To forget. Even though Mister Styron took away my sight, he didn't so much as snuff out the love-light in my heart. Some people only exist in our hearts. You know?"

"That's what you just told me," I said thinking about everything that Lettie had just told me about her Chester and Clay and her eyes. Everything. It seemed like I could scream and scream and scream for her myself all over again and again and again. I knew she still had love in her heart for them. She was like me—she didn't have anyone to talk to save for her neighbors. And maybe a stranger or two from time to time, and like Lettie, I wanted to walk much of the night to forget, but I stuck mostly to walking days.

"Come on, let's go pee," Lettie told me and motioned for me to follow her.

"I'm coming," I told her.

She led me to an outhouse. I was surprised that she never missed a step as I followed her outside. We walked along a worn path then on past a smokehouse before we stopped at a big fig tree that was directly to the right of an outhouse.

"Myra Boone, you like figs or not?"

"Oh, yes. I love figs!"

"After we pee, we can pick a few to eat while we walk and talk some more. You got any pockets?"

Eyeing me some mighty fine ripe juicy figs, "I do. You?"

"I got my apron ones—four. They plenty big to share if your pockets be small."

Knowing there was only one seat in an outhouse, "Lettie, you go first. Hear?"

"You sure?"

"I'm sure."

I figured she had to use the outhouse anyway; otherwise, she wouldn't have mentioned it. Besides, I wanted to take a closer look at the figs. See if there were any ripe ones for picking. When I moved closer to her fig tree, I saw that the crows and squirrels had helped themselves to a fig or two or more. Lots of pecks and bite marks. And it was all I could do not to reach and pick one for myself and stuff it into my mouth. I bent over and took a whiff of a fig leaf. It had a woodsy smell that reminded me of a pinch of snuff. It, too, was overloaded with some of the biggest figs I'd ever seen. I looked over at the outhouse and saw Lettie coming out. She waved at me. Smiling, "Your turn, Myra Boone. There are plenty of old newspapers for cleaning stacked up in the front left corner. Ain't no water though— unless you make it." She gave a little laugh.

"Thank you."

While inside, I still wondered if Lettie had a curse on her. And how I dare ask. When I was finished, I walked on back outside the outhouse where she was picking and loading her apron pockets with figs. Out of the corner of my left eye, I saw one blue rose bush growing directly behind the fig tree.

Suddenly, I thought to ask, "Lettie, what's your last name?"

"Stringer," she replied. Then she asked, "Why you ask me that?"

"I was just wondering. That's all."

She waved.

"Lettie, what's behind that smokehouse?"

"Myra Boone, that's my outside surprise. Saved for when I need to escape anything or anyone evil that comes my way. A neighbor found it on my property a long ago. Thought it was for sick hogs that weren't fit for smoking. Don't know for sure. Just thought so is all."

"Can I see?"

Nodding, she waved at me to walk on over.

Slowly, I walked towards the back of the smokehouse where I saw sand that was seemingly bubbling next to a little creek of sorts. "What is that?"

"Quicksand," she told me.

Never seeing such before, "What's it for?"

"Anyone or anything that be evil. Want a fig right now or not?"

Wondering, "Do you use it for the smokehouse leftover meats or what?"

"No! You run like a black runner snake be after you, and then right before you get to it, the quicksand, you take a turn and let the evil one chasing you get a 'surprise' and fall straight into it." She held out a big, ripe juicy fig for me to come and get.

I couldn't resist and walked back and took the fig from her. "If anyone or anything evil falls into it, what happens?" I put the fig in my mouth and began to chew on it. It tasted sweet and a tad green. But no matter to me, I knew I could eat a dozen or more if I got the chance. Figs made me smile.

"Once anything or anyone evil falls into the quicksand and gets scared, that scoundrel gets a big surprise!"

Nervous, "Lettie, are there any black runner snakes on your place I need to watch out for?"

"Not that I know of. Myra Boone don't cha know, a black runner won't bite you none. It chases you is all."

"Oh, I didn't know. Still, I don't want to be chased by a snake!"

Lettie giggled.

The day's sun was falling, and a full moon was rising now in Goodlife.

"Lettie Stringer, how do you keep from falling into that quicksand yourself?"

Smiling, "Mister Styron may have taken my eyes from me, but he didn't take my mind. I memorized every corner of my place. And other places too."

"How'd you do *that*?!"

Crying out, "A friend helped me before she disappeared! Besides, the stars guide me at night. That's how."

I didn't know what to say to that.

She began, "Now, Myra Boone. Let's take our walk now. And you can see for me while I listen for you to what the Lord God has in store for us tonight." She bowed her head as if to pray before shouting at me, "Shake yourself!"

"Why?"

"Shake your sins off! You got to be pure and free to see along Certainly Road. Breathe in deep—as if to clear your mind then your heart from any darkness, softly."

I obeyed her.

"Take a-hold of my right hand."

I did.

"Look up and tell me what you see."

"A full moon rising. Lettie, how are we going to see?"

"Myra Boone, you *will see* if you can believe. Be patient, hear?"

"Lettie Stringer, I'll try, but I want you to know that it's just *you and me* on this road."

Shouting, "Certainty Road!"

Sensing she was about to get mad, "Excuse me—Certainty Road."

"Myra Boone, take another fig. Chewing will help set your mind then clear it so you can carefully let it open, and we'll be on our way. Understand?"

I did as I was told. "I do. Let's hold hands, tightly."

Shouting, "Stop right now! Don't take another step or breath!" She scared me half to death.

"Why not?!"

"If you have *any* fear, we cannot walk down Certainty Road together. Take a-hold of my right hand with ease. No need to hold it tightly. Do not fear. Think about the way the water sounds when it's rolling over a rock bed at Taylor Creek. Trust me enough to put your hand in my hand. First, you've got to learn to trust. Hear?"

Without reservation, I let my right hand fall with ease into Lettie's right hand, and together we began out walk down Certainty Road—I, to be guided, in part, by the light of a full moon but more so by my willingness to learn to trust Lettie Stringer onward to a journey I never expected to take when I went to see an old blind hermit Negro woman who I was warned had a curse on her only to learn that her only curse was nothing more than making eye contact with her boss man and having love for another human on God's green earth.

"Lettie, if you don't mind me asking, what is it like to be blind?"

"When I first lost my eyes, I was at my loneliest. No one came around, even once. I learned straight away it was just me and the Lord

God," she stopped speaking as if to gather her thoughts. "I felt like a table of kitchen scraps ready to be pitched into the hog troth. Do you want to know the truth about it?"

"I do."

"I lost my feelings altogether."

"Why didn't your family and friends come and visit you? Did you move or something?"

"Lord no! How would I move?"

"What happened then? Was it on account of the curse—you smiling about nothing? That's what folks say about you, you know?"

"Myra Boone, do you want to know the truth about the truth?"

"I do."

"Kinfolk or others never show their faces around others when they got sickness or troubles—be they blind or not—because they be afraid sick folk or troubled ones will ask for something. For a dollar. For company. For a ride into town to buy victuals or dry goods. They wuz afraid I might ask them to help me wash up or pee or to bring me old newspapers..."

"*Old newspapers*?"

"For the outhouse."

"Oh."

We walked on.

"Myra Boone, a body knows in his heart when his kinfolk and others don't think about him unless they want something, like free ironing. You don't have to be blind to know that others use people that are already down on their lot in life."

I knew Lettie Stringer was telling the truth.

"You want a fig or two to chew on?" she asked me.

"Two," I answered her.

With her left hand, she reached into one of her apron pockets and brought back four figs—two for me and two for her.

I smiled.

We chewed on more figs as we continued to walk and talk straight down Certainty Road.

"Myra Boone, thank you for coming to see me. I sure am enjoying your company. Sometimes folks just need someone—someone that they can touch. It feels good for somebody to be holding my hand."

"Lettie, it feels good to me to be holding your hand too. And I mean it."

She gave my right hand a gentle squeeze that made me feel good from head to toe. I felt alive.

"Can you see?" she asked me.

"What do you mean?" I asked her.

"Can you see to walk?"

"Yes, I can see by the light of the rising moon. We are walking on moonshine. And it's real pretty too."

I felt my heart open for Lettie. It was as if the Lord God was holding up a mirror in front of me as we walked on down Certainly Road guided by the light of the moon. I realized what a sad fix she was in—blind, alone, though, strangely enough, smiling.

"Lettie, I wish you could take one of my eyes and see the moonshine," I told her.

"Myra Boone, I made my own mistakes with my life. They be nothing you can do for me. But I thank you kindly just the same for offering me one of your eyes though I'd rather have both," she said to me, popping another fig into her mouth.

I took a deep breath to keep from crying.

"Want a fig?" she asked me.

Exhaling, "Sure I do," I answered her.

She handed me a single fig. I smiled. And it wasn't the taste of the fig that brought a smile to my face either. There was something about Lettie that made me want to smile just like her even amid the night shine. I could sense that we were not alone. I felt a presence with us.

Something I've never felt before or since. Nothing I could see with my naked eyes, but it was there with us as we walked straight on.

"I'm glad you are taking a walk down Certainty Road with me," she said.

"Me too," I told her.

I looked up to see that the sky was beginning to fill with stars. More stars than I could count. The east wind whispered softly into the west. I could feel a new energy in Lettie Stringer's fingertips. I kept my word and didn't allow *any* fear to enter my mind. I tried to open it like she'd told me to do. I knew I was putting a blind trust of my own in her. I wasn't confused or uncertain at all. I felt a new loyalty enter my body to protect her too. I no longer felt like I was walking or that my heart was beating. I felt as if Lettie and I had taken flight into the newness of the night on our unexpected journey. I bowed my head, then raised it to see that we were still holding hands. I closed my eyes. When I opened my eyes, I saw that we were standing in the sky surrounded by stars. I opened and closed and opened and closed and opened and closed my eyes again and again and again to make sure that I was alive. And I was. Lettie Stringer waved at me with her left hand. And for the first time, I heard her wave. Never having heard a wave before, I smiled. She looked happy. Still blind but happy. Joyful.

I was amazed that we had travelled deep into the night and were amid the stars. We had seemingly entered another Universe—a Universe of Light.

I saw countless stars surrounding us. Some sparkled while others twinkled. I saw blue stars, red stars, crystal-clear stars, and colors that I've never seen before or since. Besides having taken an unexpected journey with Lettie, I felt as if the Lord God really did want me to learn from her how to smile, seemingly to others about nothing, especially when the darkness hit my mind the same way it hit hers when she thought back on the mistakes she'd made with and in her life.

Lettie wasn't smiling about nothing. She was smiling about everything filled with light in the Universe—His Universe of Light. I felt a stillness under my feet even though I saw nothing there. Every so often, a star would shoot out into the darkness while countless others remained steady, deliberate, and firm the same way Lettie ironed from her plain and simple kitchen when I first entered her house. Deep in my heart, I knew that she was telling me the truth. Her truth about her Chester and boy Clay with the sapphire blue eyes and what had been and hadn't been done to her because she'd made two mistakes in her life.

Lettie Stringer let go of my right hand, and her arm stretched as far as my eyes could see. With her hand she grabbed hold of a giant star, brought it back, and then offered it to me. There were no words spoken between us, yet we were bonded by an unspoken understanding I had never experienced before. When I took the star from her, I felt free from any of my earthly pain—inside and out. It was hot as fire, but in a good way. All-consuming yet comforting.

It was Lettie who spoke first, "Made for the glory of the Lord God. It will fill you with the *light of glory*. And joy. At the selfsame time, this old Negro woman lost her sight, I saw its light of glory flash throughout my mind. That much I am certain of. That's why I call this Certainty Road. Yes, I was walking down this road one night when I found myself being lifted into the sky and amid the stars. Once, I even heard a voice calling out names."

She stopped speaking as if to gather her thoughts.

"Myra Boone, I've never stopped walking at night. Folks *think* I walk alone. If the Lord God isn't walking by my side, then He sends one of his stars to guide me by night and into the day. I don't know what I'd do if I didn't have Him day in and day out. The Lord God is my eyes, my steps, my arms, my legs, my whole body! I'd be so helpless and probably throw myself into the freezing cold waters of Taylor

Creek... The *light of glory* guides this old fool Negro woman while she irons to keep her independence and tries to forget yesterday's pain."

I was unable to speak.

With what had become an endless smile, Lettie spoke, "I didn't find it; it found me. The spirit that walks and talks with me every day and night drew me here like I believe it drew you to come and see me. I am not cursed; I am blessed!"

I opened my mouth, "Lettie, can you see now?" I asked her with no effort whatsoever.

"Myra Boone, what you need to learn from me is this: The Lord God is THE bright and morning star. You can only put your trust in Him. Only Him! Be independent. He will make a way where there is no way. He will make a provision for you. That much I know to be true," she told me.

"Lettie Stringer, I thank you kindly for sharing your joy with me," I told her and reached for her right hand and put it on the star along with mine. Then, together we released the star back into the Universe of Light and all its glory before returning to walk along Certainly Road in Goodlife. Both of us smiling and sharing in a night feast of what figs she could find left in one, two, three, and then all four of her apron pockets until there were none.

ENOCH VINE

Love

The more I travelled through Goodlife to visit my neighbors, the more of an expectant climate I felt, and arriving at Mister Enoch Vine's Glass House with Margie Ann Roberts and Johnny Paul Russell was no different.

"Oh, my—Myra, would you just look at all these windows?" Margie Anne Roberts said in a marveling voice once we arrived at the Glass House. Like Mister Vine had told folks, the door was "always open" to the Glass House, so we just walked on in.

"Enter in," Mister Enoch Vine said to Margie, Johnny Paul, and me on a sunny summer afternoon.

The windows were eternal in number with some being as clear as crystal and others like jasper, only swirled with opaque colors of red, yellow, and brown. Many looked impervious to the sunlight as well as the moonlight.

Turning on both heels while looking all around the room, Johnny Paul asked, "Mister Vine, tell us where on earth did you ever get the idea for such a contraption?"

Mister Vine spun around like a top out of control before saying, "From the angel called Metatron. Yep, the Master sent His number-one Archangel to speak to me on His behalf ba-cause He knowed my small mind can't come near to understanding His majestic nature. Why, me trying to communicate with the Master on an intellectual level is like a gnat trying to drank the ocean!"

Unafraid in his presence, I smiled.

He reached for a box of Diamond kitchen matches to light the gas top. He lit the stove and placed the untouched end of the match in the right corner of his mouth and began to flick it up and down between his tongue and bottom lip. Then as a sweet color like honey entered the room, Mister Vine said, "Metatron is the Golden Flame who told me to never lose my love for others even if I remain alone and grow old and become feeble without my *one-night wife*, Baleen, or any of the Vine family, to take care of me in my last days."

"How old are you anyway?" Johnny Paul asked.

"Real old. I have yet to die like some of the others in Goodlife I have known," he stated.

Margie Anne slid her eyes from him to Johnny Paul, but neither of them said a word when their eyes locked.

Suddenly nervous, I cleared my throat.

Sensitive to the looks Margie Anne and Johnny Paul were giving him, Mister Vine said, "If you two don't want to look at me, I'll understand."

Mister Vine was thought to be the ugliest man in Goodlife. Maybe even the entire state of Mississippi. His nose was pointed like a cockroach from his stout head. His skin was dry, hollow, and black. Spotted in some places even. Long, long legs held up his flat body. Strangely enough, he looked as if he hit his knees to pray, they would transform into wings. A half dozen gray and black hairs were combed over towards the left side of his head that only held a few teeth. He had told me that his jack-o'-lantern smile was on account that his maw had spoiled him so bad because she didn't remember who his daddy was, that she didn't make him brush his teeth like everybody else.

That's what gave him his all-but-toothless smile. We had met and ate together the day of the funeral for my folks at the House of Joy and Life. And for some reason, still unbeknownst to me, I'd liked him right off.

"Mister Vine, why you so ugly?" Johnny Paul blurted out.

"Johnny Paul, that's rude!" Margie Anne was quick to shout out.

I rolled my eyes.

Pointing at me with his Jupiter finger, the jack-o'-lantern head continued, "I've already told your friend about my walk in the darkness. I can tell you two about my one-night wife and our ride on the Mississippi Queen down in New Orleans... If I've said it once, I've said it one hundred times, most folks thank ba-cause a body is ugly that he don't know he's ugly. Listen, I *know* I'm ugly, but I ain't violent about it! If you two don't want to look at me, I will understand it. It will be nothing new to me. Hell, I *know* how children have been poisoned by fairy tales. I ain't got no words of defense or spells to conjure up to save myself from my own face let alone my own skin. I may be ugly, but I'm not without feelings to the way folks can't stomach to look at me. If you want to know the truth about it, I growed up eating with the hogs. My best friend was a hog named Nanie. Me and my brother Sgt. Festus used to lay on that hog's belly to keep us warm in the winter. Oh, how we loved Nanie." Mister Vine gave a little snort that sounded like a hog gives before slopping.

Looking straight at Margie Anne and Johnny Paul, Mister Vine pushed on, "Do you two want to know more about me and the darkest of darkness that I've walked through before we go any further into the Glass House?"

Margie Anne and Johnny Paul nodded.

"My maw, Tap Lee, named me Stupid Enoch Vine. Maw marked me at birth. Set my destiny in motion from my first cry," he told them.

"Hot damn, I thought Paw's had the worst name—Russell Russell—in Goodlife," Johnny Paul said.

To my surprise, "Me too," Margie Anne agreed, then added, "Stupid is worse though."

Johnny Paul shouted and slapped his knees, "Damn right, it is!"

Again, I rolled my eyes.

Looking around, Margie Anne asked him, "Mister Vine, is your wife home?"

"Sweet Jesus, no! My one-night wife, Baleen, disappeared on me years ago one week before Christmas—on a Wednesday, December 18, to be exact. I'd already cut and fetched in a short-limbed loblolly tree from the Piney Woods."

Johnny Paul cried out, "She left you after you'd already cut down a loblolly tree?! If it'd had been me, I'd have begged her back until I got my present to open."

Margie Anne yelled out, "Johnny Paul!" She hit at him, but he ducked, and she missed.

I listened.

"She sho're as hell is hot did! Now, folks, I gots to be fair. I'm pretty much to blame for the mess I'd made of my own life before the Master sent me my own angel, Metatron, to help out with the Glass House. I had already began working on it before the first of the seven days. And long before Baleen walked through the front door of my heart and took me straight to bed. Then she hung me out, and my heart out to dry like a summer's washing. Baleen said I was *her first*, and I told her she was *my last*! I will swear on a ten-foot-tall stack of Holy Bibles that I won't EVER let a she-devil whore like her back into my life again! And if I'm lying, I'll blow my brains out like my maw did right in front of me and my brother, Sgt. Festus, who lives in Antioch, Mississippi," he confessed. He mused, "Sgt. Festus has got his own problems with the whiskey bottle, jail, and fathering children like rabbits. Not necessary in that order either!"

"I believe in angels," Margie Anne was quick to say.

"Me too," Johnny Paul agreed, then added, "But I ain't ever seen one myself. Not that I know of that is. If you know an angel, why didn't you ask it to ask God on your'n behalf to fix your'n face?"

"Sgt. Festus told me not to trouble one of God's angels with either one of our messes. That's why! Said, 'Angels are sent from the City of Light—Heaven—to purify our bodies through everything that is of good report, and no sex is involved.' While waving two balled-up fists, Sgt. Festus says to me, 'Stupid Enoch, forget Maw and whoever the hell our Paw was! Hell, it don't matter no more anyhow. If either one of them give a damn about us, they'd have treated us better than the hogs!'"

We three listened.

"Growing up, the only family I felt comfortable with was the hogs. Sgt. Festus was right about Maw and Paw. I tell you three that it is hard for me to not think about my folks. I wanted a family—a maw and a paw—other than the hogs. But it was never so," Mister Vine confessed.

Straightening her neck scarf, Margie Anne said, "I can understand that *want*," Margie Anne said.

"Me too," Johnny Paul said.

"Yeah," I mused.

Suddenly Margie Anne spoke up, "Mister Vine, my momma lost her temper on me last night and tried to choke the devil out of me."

Mister Vine shouted, "No, she didn't!"

To my surprise Margie Anne untied her red neck scarf and showed everyone her neck. It was back and blue in places and had red-like marks that resembled fingers on each side.

When we three saw Margie Anne's neck, we gasped simultaneously.

Margie Anne began to empty her heart. "Momma does this to me when daddy is off visiting his church members. I don't know *why* but she has *always* tried to kill me! It's like she hates my guts! Momma has never loved me. I've never felt her love for one day in my entire life. Only my daddy's love and stranger's love have I felt." She stopped speaking and looked at me and Johnny Paul before saying, "I know Myra Boone loves me too. She loves everyone the same. I know that Johnny Paul "likes me," and that's enough. He's still my best friend, as far as a boy goes."

Johnny Paul walked over and reached for Margie Anne's scarf, and he gently began to tie it very tidy-like back around her neck to hide her bruises. He never said a word. He just smiled at her and nodded. For some strange reason, they unexpectedly looked like twins to me.

Moving towards Mister Vine, Margie Anne continued, "I told you about my momma, so you'd know that life isn't always easy even if you have a momma," Margie Anne said while piercing her bottom lip with her eye teeth.

Johnny Paul shouted out, "You damn right!"

Strangely enough, Mister Vine smiled at me, and I smiled back.

"Mister Vine, you want a paw, do ya? Since I was knee-high to a jackrabbit, my maw told me my number-one job was to look after mine. From sunup to sundown. Forget going to the schoolhouse to read the dic-tion-ary or look at pretty picture books or colorful road maps. Forget swimmin' and eatin' ice-cold watermelon or fishin' on Saturdays in Taylor Creek with the other children," Johnny Paul said before looking around the Glass House. "You still pining for a maw and a paw livin' in a bea-u-ti-ful house like this? You told us right off, you had an angel come help you out... If you ask me, then you ought to have your'n head examined by Doc Farmer!"

To my surprise, Margie Anne shouted, "Amen!"

Removing the match from his mouth, Mister Vine responded, "I guess you both are speaking truth into this ugly ole' fool-headed man's life. The Glass House *has become* my earthly abode of bliss. I'm safe here. And my door is always open for anyone that wants to share in its beauty."

"Mister Vine, I thank you kindly for letting me and my friends come by to visit without letting you know that we were coming to see the Glass House," I said to him.

Margie Anne and Johnny Paul were watching him close.

"Well, you can thank me all you want, but it was the Master who reached down and tapped you, Myra Boone, on the shoulder to come visit a neighbor with your friends today," Mister Vine told us.

Margie Anne and Johnny Paul exchanged glances.

Believing him, I felt my lips begin to quiver, my eyes welling up with tears.

Mister Vine looked at me. "God's strength is made perfect in your weakness," he said.

Johnny Paul saved me from crying with, "Mister Vine, we thank you for lettin' us come just the same."

Margie Anne nodded in total Roberts' agreement. She pushed her thick glasses back up onto her nose and straightened her scarf.

"Mister Vine, what kind of glass is this?" I asked, looking at a stone-like glass.

Pointing to the North, he explained, "This here's a jasper window, and next to it is a sapphire glass which come all the way from Italy. The other glasses are everything from chalcedony to emerald to sardonyx. And, I have chrysolite and beryl stone-like glass. Topaz is next to a sheet of chrysoprase directly beside rare jacinth."

Margie Anne gasped in awe.

Reaching into his pocket and pulling out a tube of ChapStick, he shouted out, "And my favorite—amethyst!"

"You don't say so?" Johnny Paul asked.

He gave us a satisfied look, uncapped the ChapStick, and while sweeping his bottom lip twice, he mused, "John Shows give me the amethyst. Said it helps with the healing of the earthly body."

"I'm not surprised," Margie Anne commented.

When I nodded, I felt my tears vanish.

Johnny Paul cleared his throat and asked, "Mister Vine, why are some windows see-through and others are not see-through?"

Cutting off the gas-top stove, he told us, "Ba-cause in this old world, it don't matter if the sun shines or if the moon glows ba-cause—."

"How's that?" Margie Anne asked.

"The Master gives the light," he mused and motioned for us to follow him.

"Mister Vine, how many windows are there?" Johnny Paul asked.

"Twelve in all."

"Do tell," Margie Anne observed.

"Let's all go outside," he instructed us.

We followed Mister Vine out the front door in a straight line, me first.

Once outside, I saw that a mist of sweat had covered Mister Vine's brow. He looked like he was nothing more than a stick of wax ready to melt under a sun that was starting to set.

"Mister Vine, why are you still so sad? Why, I just bet that this is the most beautiful house in the world. And it's all yours. You don't have to share it with anyone! What's wrong?" I asked him.

"Sssshush!" Johnny Paul told me.

Margie Anne punched him to hush.

Mister Vine said, "Like I told you, I wasted all my love on a foreign wife that I can't get out of my head."

"Haven't you got any more love inside you to give away?" I asked.

No one made a sound.

Mister Vine took three steps back, closed his eyes, rolled his neck around on his shoulders, and looked towards the sky whispering, "I'm an admitted rascal. But I turned from my wicked ways. I have reached up and took the Master's hand though I've hardly ever crossed my pride line to tell very many souls on this earth that I love them. And if you only knew what trouble that has caused me all of my life."

"Why not?" I asked him.

"Ba-cause I've always felt like an ugly *Nobody*—a good-for-nothing, ugly *Nobody*! By giving me Stupid for a first name, my maw hammered into everyone's head, including mine, that I would never be worth a hill of beans. And I believed her—from day one. Then one day, I was give the gift of my Baby. Yes, when Baby wandered up to the Glass House, I crossed my pride line and accepted the Master's grace and mercy and love. I guess you could say that I'm a work in progress. I may never finish my earthly living until I cross over to the other side into Glory."

I shouted, "Baby?!"

Mister Vine nodded and seemingly faded out of our sight.

Again shouting, I told him, "Enoch, not a soul in Goodlife has any earthly idea you have *a baby* to take care of! Where'd you go? Enoch?!"

A dog began to sing.

"What in the world?" Margie Anne asked the sky.

Johnny Paul looked north, south, east, and west.

Fading back into our sight, Mister Vine shouted, "That's Baby."

A large African dog joined us. Instead of barking, the dog sang in little choppy notes while bouncing its head with confidence. The dog was missing one toe from its left paw and was sporting a gold tooth.

"Sing, Baby, sing for our company," Mister Vine told the dog.

Baby sang, "Raurl-raurl-raurl, rarlaaarlrlrlaaarl. Raurl-raurl-raurl, rarlaaarlrlrlaaarl. Raurl-raurl-raurl, rarlaaarlrlrlaaarl."

"Why is that dog a-singin'?" Johnny Paul asked him.

"Baby sings. She hasn't ever barked once since Elohim sent her to guide me along my way. She is just an old singing beast of a dog. Baleen hated Baby right off! That should have given me my first hint Baleen was up to no good."

"Who is Elohim?" I asked.

"God," he replied.

"Of all things," Margie Anne marveled.

Johnny Paul laughed.

And with Mister Enoch Vine's last two words, no more words were spoken between us three about the Glass House. As the evening sun fell into the west, Enoch reached down and took Baby into his arms.

At first, the African singing dog gave its earthly Master a struggle until he crossed his pride line and whispered, "I love you." And it was then that man and beast became one amid the light of the fallen sun.

UNCLE JOHN SHOWS

Grace

The May honeysuckle vines were smelling like cotton candy as they presented Margie Anne Roberts and me with a carpet of tiny, fresh blooms to walk upon. The path we walked down to get to Uncle John's house was narrow, and it must have been walked on for hundreds of years by the harvesters of the land.

After about a quarter of a mile or so, I saw Uncle John's house hidden in the Piney Woods. I could see a pink crape myrtle tree sheltering it from the sunlight as well as a weeping willow tree that he had ordered from New Orleans seemingly holding onto the sides of the house with its long, flowing limbs. I looked to see if he'd put in any more amethyst windowpanes that he was so fond of on account of them promoting healing, but I only saw the half a dozen or so in a side window that he'd been working on before he fell sick.

"Look how beautiful it is here," Margie Anne remarked as we headed towards the front porch.

"Margie Anne, I might as well tell you that Uncle John really isn't my uncle. My grandfolks brought him into the family years and years ago. He had no one to care about him. He was a good and kind worker," I told her.

She threw me a quizzical look, "What kind of a worker?"

"He took care of folk's yards and did any odd job they offered him to make ends meet. He loves putting in glass windows too," I replied to her then added, "Many have shared their daily food and Sunday dinners with him for years too."

Smiling, "There is nothing wrong with that," she said.

"One other thing—Uncle John has high yellow skin. He's a Negro with light skin," I told her.

"There is nothing wrong with that either," she said. She pushed her thick glasses back up on her nose.

I stopped her and asked, "Margie Anne, have you ever seen anybody with the cancer and all before?"

Again, pushing her thick glasses back up on her nose, she thought and then answered, "No, I don't think that I have. But I have been visiting the Ellisville State School for the mentally retarded with my daddy and all for years. Is it like that or something?"

"Nope. Not even close," I said. "Margie Anne, Uncle John is suffering with a real bad disease and all of its sorrows, not sick in the head like the poor folks over at the Ellisville State School are. Why, those folks were born mentally retarded or such. Uncle John has never been mentally retarded a day in his entire life. He is in pain in a serious way—that's for sure. So, I might as well tell you that he is not a pretty sight to see. Have you ever seen a dead dog after a car has run over him?"

"Of course, I have! And I have often wondered why the dog's family never came to look for him," she said, looking a little nervous.

"Well, the cancer is like a dead dog that has been two or more days laying in the hot, scorching sun. At least Uncle John's is anyway because he has cancer of the face from smoking all those Pall Mall cigarettes," I warned her.

"Mary Myra Boone, my daddy is a preacher man, and I have heard it all, I dare say. And besides that, me and my brother, Michael, have buried many a dead dog," she bragged.

"Well, you may have *heard* it all, but I doubt if you have *seen* it all."

"Just don't act afraid of him because he won't hurt you or no one else. He looks awful bad because he is about eat up with sorrow."

Shaking her head up-and-down with confidence, Margie Anne said, "Oh, Myra, I won't be afraid of him. I know all about sick folks and have even read about how the Lord was hung on a cross with nails in Him. So, I won't be afraid."

"Well, Uncle John is different from anything or anyone that you have ever seen or read about before. That's all I have to say."

Please Lord don't let anyone be filled with fear or hurt today.

Approaching the screen door of his front porch, I looked up above the door and saw flies fiercely swarming around its cracks. There were hundreds of them making the most awful noise that you could ever imagine. They sounded like they were speaking real words but, in another language, like a dark voice or such absent from any light whatsoever.

Let us in, let us in, let us in... We want to go inside with you, said a dark voice. *Death is near, death is near here—just around the corner. We are here for him, we are here.*

We walked up on the front porch to knock on the screen door. Those flies didn't even seem to notice us or the food that we were carrying. I proceeded to knock on the door loudly, until I heard a tired voice say, "Come on in. It's open."

Calling out amid the creaking sound of the screen door, "It's Myra, Uncle John. I got a friend with me—the preacher's baby girl, Margie Anne Roberts."

"Praise be! Company!" he shouted.

About that time, I turned towards Margie Anne, who looked like she was going to faint. She was apparently trying to figure out why all the flies were eagerly wanting to go inside the house.

"Do you still want to go in?"

"Of course, I do."

When we entered the house, Uncle John began to scream out as the flies swarmed all around us, "For God's sake, don't let them flies in! Aaahuhuahah! Oh, my Law'd, they ain't nothing but tools of the Devil and they seek to torment me as I lay here on my death bed. Aaahuhuahah, help me! Get 'em away from my face!"

"Margie Anne, come on in here quick," I said.

She about broke her neck to get in the narrow crack that I was making in the screen door for her to run through. But some of the flies did get in and flew straight towards the open rotting flesh on Uncle John's face.

"Aaahuhuahah, Father, help me! Have mercy on me and stop them Devil flies from persecuting me!" he screamed out.

He was a frail old man who looked like he only ate about once a day. Right in the center of his face, where his nose once was, I saw an open hole that had some Jergens lotion dabbed around it. I could only make out about half of what used to be his whole nose. All I could think about was that the center of his face looked like a T-bone steak does before cooking. He had all his hair though. And he didn't have a gray hair in his head. I was worried that if he fell out of his sickbed that he would break slam in two.

The earth shook and the sky roared with thunder and lightning. "*Eli, Eli, lama sa-bach-tha-ni?*" Uncle John cried out in a loud voice while the earth continued to shake. I knew from church it meant *My God, My God, why hast thou forsaken me?*

What in the world does he mean by saying such a thing?

I felt my eyes almost pop out of my head as he began to swing his arms from right to left in midair, grabbing those flies with his pure hands as they swarmed all around him. He would catch one, squeeze it, throw it as far as he could, only to have to catch another and do the same. The flies that he couldn't catch quickly enough landed right onto what was left of his ol' nose.

"Aaahuhuahah, Law'd God, forgive me! Don't let the Devil have his way with me any longer!" he screamed out as his voice echoed a house that held the smell of death from top to bottom.

I grabbed the fly swatter and began to hit at some of the flies.

Margie Anne stood in the corner of the room holding her hands in a prayerful style praying, "In the name of Jesus, get out of this house—NOW!"

She is doing what Brother Jim taught her.

For one moment, I saw the pain in Uncle John's worn-down face jump out like a wave of fear. I had to duck to keep it from getting on me. It circled the room like a spirit or such smiling at me before reentering his face causing him to cry out louder. Suddenly, I knew for the first time what my granddaddy had meant when he said that we all have a cross to bear in our lives when we would talk about Momma, Daddy, and Great Aunt Annabelle dying in the Merrihope fire and all. And I figured that Uncle John's cross was the cancer.

I noticed a little metal fan in the corner by the couch. I ran and turned it on, and at the same time Margie Anne came to help me and pointed it in the direction of his bed to blow those devil flies *off* or at least *away* from his face.

I saw the wind take the flies away from his face. He began to get some relief from their gnawing at not only his flesh but at his peace as well. After a few minutes, when he had crushed all of the flies, he could get his hands on, or the Good Lord had heard Margie Anne's prayer, or both, I watched the room clear of those filthy, nasty winged insects that were trying to persist in eating him alive.

With relief he cried out, "Thank you, Father!"

Margie Anne and I exchanged glances.

In an exhausted but clear Southern voice, he said, "Now, *please,* Girls, would you let me rest a few minutes. Would one of you go into the kitchen and git me the water pitcher and a wet rag so that I can sponge off my face and clean up some? Put a little vinegar in the wash bowl if you don't mind—it's in the cabinet next to the icebox."

"Yes, Sir!" our voices echoed in the room in unison, and we both ran towards the kitchen.

I looked around and saw hundreds of flies around the tops and along the sides of the windows throughout his house. I could hear their buzzing and tried to put the idea out of my mind as to what their voices might be saying, but I could still hear their dark voices ring through my mind, continuing to ask for Uncle John's soul while he washed off their blood.

We are here and we will never stop until he is ours. Let us in, let us in. We are here for him. Let us take him to Sheol now. The time is now for us to take him away. Death is just around the corner, rang all through my mind from their dark voices.

"Come on over here my pretty girl and let me look at you," Uncle John said.

I shook my head to clear it from the dark voices.

Reaching out to take the bloody dishrag from his hand, "Which one of us pretty girls are you talking about?" Margie Anne teased.

"Why, the *both* of you!" he said, throwing the wet, bloody rag into the washbowl with relief. The smell of vinegar filled the room for a short while.

We just laughed and pretended not to notice what a fix he was in.

"Hey there, *neighbor!*" Margie Anne said enthusiastically.

"Hey back, *Silvergirl!* And just look at you, Myra Boone—if you don't look exactly like your momma, Marigold, did when she was your age, I don't know who does. My goodness, gracious alive! Ain't you tall?"

"I suppose."

"And I declare if you don't have pretty hair—almost the golden color of autumn—I don't know who does," he said while I began unpacking our Sunday dinner with the hopes that he would tell us a story or two even though he was as weak as any Mississippi red-orange clay that I had ever seen around a freshly dug grave. I knew in my heart that his stories would stay with me like those stained-glass windows over at the church that it took him ten or more years to put in by looking at a picture of the chapel windows at that *Duke University* would stay—for the rest of my life.

When I looked up over the mantle, I saw a little piece of wood that someone had cut from a pine tree in the shape of the sun with the words carved around it to represent the sun's rays: *Faith can break the sky in two and let the Face of God shine through.* There was a single hand in its middle and a blue rose in the center of the hand. I took Margie Anne by the hand, and we walked boldly together towards the sight that the good Lord had placed before us.

"Oh, my God! My nose is killing me—Aaahuhuahah!" Uncle John cried out in pain.

I turned to Margie Anne and saw that she had the look of fear spread across her face, but she never said so much as an unkind word to him. Instead, she cleared her throat, took a deep breath, coughed, and said, "Let's just fix our plates, and then maybe your Uncle John can tell us a story or two. Would you tell us a story?"

"I reckon so," he said, sitting up from his sick bed.

We began to unpack the paper sack that Grandma Davis had packed slam full of fried chicken and such.

"Silvergirl, would you go into the kitchen and get me that red and green bed tray with the poinsettias painted on top of it?" he asked Margie Anne.

Margie Anne cheerfully obliged him without question and skipped into the other part of the house singing all the while. *Who called the Preacher to come a-prayin'? Billy Boy, yes, Billy Boy! Who called the Doctor to come a-doctorin'? Billy Boy, yes, Billy Boy! If you're saved and you know it say, Billy Boy, yes, Billy Boy! If you're saved and you know it say, Billy Boy, yes, Billy Boy!*

"What in the world is that child singing?" he asked.

I shook my head with pure amazement at how Margie Anne could find *any* words to sing after what she and I had just witnessed, let alone skip merrily through a house that had nothing left in it to inspire her but the pure smell of death itself. "I suppose she is acting that way—happy and all—because she feels like she is tending to you like a nurse or something. She wants to be a nurse when she grows up, I think. And maybe she thinks that she will set up her practice with you first!" I teased him.

"Well, she can sing, dance, or even cook if that makes her happy, but she ain't stickin' nary nursing needle in no part of this here body!" he shot back at me, tucking the napkin into his pajama shirt—ready to eat, no doubt. "Doc Farmer has been tending me for nearly thirty-seven years. And mind you, I ain't looking to replace him or his mare!" he said like he had the faith of Job in Doc Farmer.

"Lord-a-mercy, Uncle John! Are you scared of needles?" I teased him once again, hoping for a smile.

Margie Anne came into the room with his poinsettia bed tray. She danced around the bed and set it right down in front of him, pretending not to notice his face and all. He looked with total amazement at her and then over towards me. I thought I'd have a little fun and tease them both a little.

"The joy of the Lord is your strength—did you know that *neighbor?*" she asked him.

"You bet I do! Silvergirl, how old are you anyway?" he asked, slumping back down in his bed.

"Twelve—June 25th, that is," she replied.

"How long you been wearing them thick glasses?"

"My eyes have been dim pretty much since birth. So, I reckon, for about as long as I can remember."

"About dim, eh? *You don't mean it!*" he marveled, sitting up to get a better look at her.

With a smile she told him, "Yes. *Dim*, not blind though. There is a difference, you know?"

Smiling back at her while in warm agreement, "Oh, I know there is."

"And sometimes, I can see better than other times."

"Sure enough?"

"Yep."

"Margie Anne, did you pick up your pack of needles for giving shots and all from George Wilkerson's drug store yesterday when you went into town with your folks?" I teased.

She smiled over my way.

"Silvergirl, come closer. I'll show you what gives me my joy," Uncle John said, reaching under his pillow. He pulled out something.

"What you got?" I asked, stepping closer to his bed for fear that maybe he had hidden his gun under his head in case of trouble. But when he opened up his hand, out fell a small piece of wood that smelled of sandlewood.

Margie Anne reached down, picked it up, and read aloud, "*Jerusalem*. Look right here, Myra," she said with amazement, and her eyes grew twice in size behind her thick glasses.

"What in the world is it?" I asked.

"It's a piece of the *Cross*," Uncle John said proudly.

"*What Cross?*" I asked him.

"The pure *Cross*—the one that Jesus was hung on!" Margie Anne proclaimed loudly. She looked towards Uncle John while he nodded his head up-and-down with as much honesty as you would ever expect to see from a self-made Mississippi yardman.

"Yes, it surely is," he said.

"Oh, go on!" I said, knowing what they both meant but not willing to believe it.

"It is, it is, it surely is!" Margie Anne continued to proclaim while he nodded in total agreement with her.

"*I recognize it*," she whispered to him.

"*I figured you would*," he whispered back.

"How in the world did you ever get *that*?" I asked, still wanting to believe but couldn't.

"That George Wilkerson over at the drugstore give it to me. He got it in Durham, North Carolina, when he was studying how to fill prescriptions at that *Duke University*. He assured me that it was the real thing," he said like he was Saint Peter preaching the gospel.

"Jesus Christ!" Margie Anne cried out.

George Wilkerson owned the drugstore in Soso over on Appletree Street right next to the Better Living Grocery Store. Even though not one soul in Goodlife let alone Soso could pronounce its name, "Eruditio et Religio," no one cared because they trusted George to always do the right thing by them. Everybody loved George because he had done went and gone off to college over in North Carolina for about four or so years. And that made him *well traveled* as far as everyone was concerned. No one ever doubted a single thing that he told them. Besides, he would give them credit as well as extra refills sometimes. Everyone was as loyal to him as he was to them.

"Then why did he *give it to you?*" I asked, looking deep into his marred face.

He smiled from us to the piece of wood, like it had some sort of power over him.

Margie Anne stood there smiling from ear to ear.

"To save my life! George said that the Lord God would have wanted me to have this because I was in such pain and all. Besides, the Dem-e-rol isn't working anymore, and my refills are all used up—including my extras," he said, offering it out to us for proper inspection.

"Well, look at this," I said to Margie Anne.

She moved in closer, holding the fried chicken plate.

"Why, it has a piece of scrap iron with letters engraved it its center, *Jerusalem*," I read aloud again, and we all began to fix our plates.

"*Mercy!*" Margie Anne proclaimed. Shaking her head from side to side in total Roberts' amazement she stated," I would like to have me a piece of the *Cross* myself to take around with me in my front pocket or in my purse or just to hold on to in times of trouble like when Momma loses her temper on me—that's for sure."

"Your momma got a bad temper, eh?" Uncle John asked.

"She sure does."

"I hate to hear that—a bad temper can be an awful thing to have to put up with."

"Tell me about it."

Suddenly, what Margie Anne had said hit me like a truckload of bricks. "What do you mean you *recognize* it?"

"Well, Myra, when Momma beats what *she* calls 'a rebellious spirit' out of me, I have to pray double hard because sometimes I can hardly bear it. Many times, I fall on off to sleep, and I have this dream every time about Jesus hanging on the Cross. I tell Him how I feel, and I simply imagine that I put my head on His side—the side with the spear wound in it. When I wake up, I feel better. And this here piece of wood looks like it could very well be the same *exact* wood in my dream. Yes! It's the same kind of wood. What I'd like to know is how did George Wilkerson got hold of a piece of the Cross?"

"I knew it! I knew it! I knew it was *gen-u-ine*! Silvergirl, bless your sweet heart for the long-awaited confirmation! But I do hate to hear that you have to put up with such at your house."

No wonder she's always sitting on Go.

"I endure—that's for sure."

"Doesn't your sister, Sharon Rose, or your brother, Michael, ever take up for you?" I asked her.

"Nope. Momma done gone and run them off—it's only me, Daddy, and her. And, of course, my books," she said sadly, pushing her thick glasses back up onto her nose. She took in a deep breath and smiled at us while straightening her pretty chiffon neck scarf.

Mercy! What good can books do her?

"Did George Wilkerson tell you where he got the piece of Cross wood from or not?" Margie Anne asked.

"Well, all I know is that he said that one of those professors over at Trinity University—I mean *Duke*—brung it back from overseas or something of that nature. And he assured me it was *precious* wood. Here, smell it," he said proudly. His face began to shine, no longer looking marred from the cancer.

"Goodness gracious alive! I ain't never heard of such," I said.

"Has it helped you any yet?" Margie Anne asked him, ever so sincerely.

We both took a whiff of the wood.

"I reckon it has—mostly its words," he said.

"What *words?* I only saw one word: *Jerusalem*," I wondered what I had missed.

"*Silvergirl*, here, take it. Turn it over and read it for Myra."

"Y-H-W-H," she spelled, then said, "Mercy, it sure smells right good, doesn't it?"

"What in the world does Y-H-W-H spell?" I asked them.

"That there is one of the Lord God's most precious names. Yep. All you got to do to make it a word is to add an *a* and an *e*, and then you get *Yahweh*," he said, taking the piece of wood back from me.

Then he replaced it underneath his pillow like it was a gun or something.

"What had does *Yahweh* mean?" I asked.

"Why, it's the most holy name in the Good Book! It simply means: "I Am—I Am that I Am. And since," he began to tell us, "Jerusalem is the capital city of Israel that patiently sits on a high ridge slam west of the Dead Sea and the River Jordan—I mean Jordan River! It stands for *pure* holiness in my book because it is *the* scene of Jesus' last ministry as well as where they keep the heavenly—I mean heavily—guarded Church of the Holy Sepulcher," he proclaimed much to my surprise.

"Great Day in the Morning! And that sepulcher is sure enough holy because it is where they placed the body of *my* Jesus after they crucified Him on the Cross. It's sort of a tomb in the earth, isn't it?" Margie Anne asked.

"It is indeed! And it was the very city of Jerusalem that *my* Lord and Savior walked many a mile in, not to mention His faithful servant David and his boy, the wisest man that ever lived, old King Solomon. Why, they walked many a mile in order to carry out their missions while they were in this old world. Why, Jerusalem was the place to *be* once upon a time," he informed us both without blinking an eye.

"Brother John, do you think that it helps you, *really?*" Margie Anne asked him.

"Oh, sweet girls, I guess it's because I think of how Jesus hung on the Cross without so much as a whimper one. When I think that He did it for just for me, I must admit that I get encouraged about dying," he confessed.

"*About dying?*" we echoed.

He nodded.

"I sure do!"

"What piece of fried chicken do you want?" Margie Anne cut in, finally holding up an easy-breezy blue crystal plate.

"I want the breast if they is one," Uncle John said with some excitement for his lunch. "Have you got any sweet corn in there? I know your Grandma Reatha makes the best sweet corn in this part of the country."

"Well, give me the wing," I said, noticing for the first time the colorful Christmas lights that were strung up and blinking across the mantle and draped over the head of every door in his house.

"Good, I get the leg!" Margie Anne said. She tossed a breast then a thigh onto Uncle John's poinsettia bed tray.

"Yep, there's an oyster pint jar packed slam full of sweet corn in here," I said, hoping we wouldn't fight over it because I knew how good we all loved it.

"Getting on back to the comfort that the Cross offers me about dying," Uncle John continued like we hadn't butted in on him.

"Do you all want any of this potato salad or not?" Margie Anne asked us.

"Margie Anne, give us all a little bit of everything and let Uncle John get on with his story! And hand me a piece of that Little Miss Sunbeam White Bread," I said, about to get aggravated.

"All-rightie then," she said, as kind as a kitten, but without ever looking over at me because she was too busy looking into the brown paper bag.

Taking a bite out of his chicken breast like he hadn't eaten in a year or two, Uncle John continued on with, "I can keep an eye on the Holy Land."

"Have you had a *vision* or what?" Margie Anne asked him and looked around before she marveled, "My goodness gracious alive, it sure looks like Christmas in here, doesn't it?"

We had been so involved in looking and listening to him talk that we hadn't even noticed the inside of his house or its contents. But she was right because he or somebody had decorated the entire place to look and feel like Christmas every day of the year, no doubt about it. And to come to think of it, it did *look* a great deal like Christmas, but it certainly didn't *feel* like Christmas that was for sure.

There was a shiny, aluminum Christmas tree in the corner of his bedroom and one in the corner of the front parlor. Neither tree had any ornaments though—like you'd expect to see hanging from the limbs of a Christmas tree—both trees were as bare as a newborn baby. But the colorful lights that were strung up all over the place seemed to make up for it because they made his entire house look like a perfect rainbow.

"Law'd have mercy, not me! I ain't ever had one of them *visions* like you— yet," he laughingly said.

We both sat down on a settee that looked like a candy cane in December because he had covered it with the most beautiful red and white silk-like material that I had ever laid my eyes on. "Where did you get this red and white material from?" I asked.

"Jackson," he answered me. "I simply mean that I can or that I have made my choice or wish known to God about what I want as soon as I get into the Promised Land—Heaven—that is."

"Tell us, then," I said, all the while wondering where all this was going. When as I got up and fed him a spoonful of the potato salad, I noticed that Margie Anne was eating her pineapple-raisin upside-down cake *first*.

For somebody who claims to be allergic to sweets, she sure doesn't act like it any more than my Granddaddy Davis does.

Chewing his potato salad while crying out in pain, "Aaahuhuahah! My poor ol' nose about kills me every time I try to eat a bite!" Before requesting, "Give me a little of that sweet corn if you don't mind."

I obliged him.

Taking a deep breath, he said ever so tenderly, "I want to ride a white horse by the River of Life when I look towards the City of God or Heaven for your Aunt Lois Anne." He looked over towards Margie Anne who was eating like she was starving.

"Now that is really nice, if I do say so myself," Margie Anne said, stuffing a raisin back into her piece of cake that had fell out on the rush up to her mouth.

"She was my *Lamb*. And if she hadn't died giving birth to our only son, John Davis, Jr., I wouldn't have smoked all them Pall Mall cigarettes. I believe that they give me this cancer," he said with a wispy voice.

"Why in the world did her dying make you smoke Pall Mall cigarettes of all things?" I asked him.

"I know *exactly* why," Margie Anne said confidently and then added, "His nerves and all."

"Well, Margie Anne, everybody's got nerves and all," I said shortly.

"I know *that*. But some folks have got more nerves to keep calmed down than others do. Daddy says that it depends on what a body has been through when it comes to treating or calming down the nerves and all."

"Myra, now she's part right," he said in total agreement shaking his head up-and-down while moaning ever so loudly. "Aaahuhuahah! Oh me, oh my! My ol' nose is about to fall slam off my face!"

"And my daddy told me that some folks take to drinking whiskey as well. Do you drink?"

"Law'd no! I ain't never touched the stuff."

"Well, that's something to be thankful for right there!"

"Silvergirl, you something else. You know it?" he said, smiling at Margie Anne who smiled back while pushing her thick glasses back up onto her nose.

"Uncle John, tell us—just tell us, what do you want us to do for you, you hear?"

"There ain't nary a thang to do but pray because I am too far gone for anything else. And it ain't nobody's fault but my own that I didn't love my body enough to take better care than to fill it up with tobacco smoke — and nic-o-tine," he informed us.

"Well, my daddy told me that folks smoke because they are nervous or hooked or both," Margie Anne said.

"Well, he's pretty much right," Uncle John agreed.

"See, I was left heartbroken after my Lois Anne died, and then the boy up and died in my arms four days later to boot. I don't know how I ever made it alone for so many years," he continued, taking another bite out of his chicken breast.

Walking over to a small, humble-looking plant, Margie Anne asked, "What kind of a plant is this?"

"Hyssop. It's mostly for purifying my lungs and such," he said.

His face is not shining like it was shining when he was holding onto that of piece of wood.

"Where did you get it?" she asked, eyeing the plant.

"Raven brought it. It was a gift from some of the People of The Way that live over towards Brother Jalla's church."

Margie Anne and I exchanged glances when we heard him talk of Raven and The Way.

"Well, I'll be dog. I don't think I've ever seen such a plant—hyssop, eh?"

"Yep."

"Myra, do you reckon that this plant would help your bronchitis any?" she asked.

"I doubt it. Now, Uncle John, you were not alone," I said, taking in a deep breath. Then, I kissed him on the cheek because I wanted him to know without a shadow of a doubt that I loved him no matter what shape he was in. "You gave all of your life to serving the Lord and your friends at the Union Community Church. *Everyone* knows what a *fine* yardman you are. And your storybook stained glass windows are beautiful."

His face lit up like a Christmas tree.

"*Grace* is the most *powerful* voice of all," Margie Anne interrupted with for whatever the reason then added. "And from where I see it, the Lord has certainly given you plenty of it—that's for sure!"

He looked at her briefly and back to me like he was thinking about what she had said. He just smiled and pointed to a stone-like plaque that was hanging directly over the front door. It read *Tabernacle of the Congregation.*

"Where in the world did you get *that* old thing from?" I asked, wondering if I should read it aloud so Margie Anne wouldn't feel left out. But I didn't.

"Oh, I've had it ever since I can remember—about 430 years or so. Moses left it behind," he answered with a smile.

Music began to play.

"Is that the television?" Margie Anne asked.

"Silvergirl, what time is it?" he asked.

"Almost 2:30," she said, looking at her wristwatch.

"*Hereboy! Hereboy!* Git on in here as fast as you can!" he called out, and with his words in bounced a scrawny old hound dog. The old hound dog didn't even give us a second look; instead, it parked itself down at the foot of Uncle John's sickbed and smiled.

"Where did you get the new dog?" I asked.

"He wandered up here last week. And I took a vote as to whether he could stay or not, and he was voted in!"

The hound dog barked, "Auuhuh rarara, ruff! Auuhuh rarara, ruff!"

"Who voted?" I asked him.

The hound dog glanced over my way like he had a measure of understanding.

"Me and him!" he said.

Once again, Margie Anne fell back on the settee laughing.

"Ain't that right, Hereboy?" he asked the hound dog.

"Auuhuh rarara, ruff! Auuhuh rarara, ruff!" the hound dog replied.

"What's his name?" I asked.

"Hereboy. Didn't you hear me call him? Give him them chicken scraps and anything that was left from that *fine* dinner so that he can get on back in yonder to watch his favorite TV show. He was the one who turned on the television. He watches "Mutual of Omaha's Wild Kingdom." It's almost three o'clock and Sunday, ain't it?"

Again, the hound dog smiled at him.

"Give him the bones and all," he ordered.

"Margie Anne, what are you whispering to him?" I asked.

"I'm showing him my wristwatch. That's all. But he isn't too interested in Time."

Walking back into the bedroom, she asked my uncle, "Have you got anything sweet we can snack on?"

"Margie Anne, Uncle John's got the *Sugar Diabetes*, so he can't keep sweets around," I informed her.

"I surely do! And if you'll go in yonder and look in the icebox and bring me that blue coffee can along with a couple of spoons, I'll be happy to share my own private gold stock of homemade stock of sweet stuff with you," he told her.

"Huh?" I asked.

Margie took off towards the kitchen and returned with a blue coffee can and three tarnished silver spoons.

"Good girl!" he praised her.

She smiled as big as the Mississippi River while rocking her head east to west.

"Now, open the lid," he instructed.

"What in the world?" I asked.

"Taste it and see if you like it."

"Not unless you tell me what it—," I said.

"I will," Margie Anne spoke up and stuck her spoon into the coffee can and filled it with gold-like sparkles and ate it like she was starving.

"*It's wonderful!*" she proclaimed and gave him a little taste.

With satisfaction, "I knew you would like it!" Then he cried out, "Aaahuhuahah! Aaahuhuahah! Oh, my Law'd, my face hurts!"

"Myra, what do you think of it?" Margie Anne asked me, ignoring him.

"Uncle John, would you just tell me what it is first?"

"Pure sugar, fresh butter, and sifted flour all dashed with brown sugar and a touch of cinnamon, but chilled to perfection. I call it *Delight*," he told me.

Going for another spoon of the gold, Margie Anne proclaimed, "I just *love* homemade sweet stuff!"

Uncle John cried out, "*Hosanna, Silvergirl, Hosanna!*"

Margie Anne clapped her hands twice.

I walked over to the window where the flies were still swarming around the outside of the house trying to come inside with us. That's when I looked up and saw a big steady hand reach down from the sky and gently slide underneath the foundation of the house. And when I turned to tell Margie Anne to come and see the big hand, a voice spoke to my heart and simply said, *Listen*. I obeyed the voice, but it never spoke again. Then I saw something that had the likeness of a cloud enter the house from the floor on up to the ceiling, and I began to feel like a small family picture hanging on a wall while I listened to Margie Anne continue to encourage her new-found neighbor on with words filled with nothing but pure love while the cloudlike image slowly disappeared into the walls of Uncle John's house.

RAVEN

The Secret of Life

"*Scuttles and cans, buttons and bows. I'll cure your ills, and I'll cheer your woes,*" sang a sweet voice as clear as a whippoorwill as Margie Ann Roberts and I fought through the thick green Piney Woods of Goodlife in search of Raven and The Way.

"That must be *her*. We were told to pass Uncle John Shows' place and listen for a song. Remember?" Margie Anne reminded me, looking all around, while pushing her thick glasses back up onto her nose.

"Sounds like a Sunday peddler working his way through the Piney Woods," I observed.

A small, dark-skinned, skinny girl stepped out from behind a weeping willow tree. She was about four feet tall with long, curly black hair. Her eyes were sapphire blue.

"My name is Raven," she said, giving us a quick, shy smile without making eye contact.

"What kind of name is *Raven?*" Margie Anne asked.

Looking down shyly at her bare feet, "Poppa gave it to me after Maw flew off with some salesman named Jude Murphy. Jude's the one who taught me the song. Yep. Poppa changed my name right before he went and put me out on my own," she told us.

"What do you mean by 'put me out on my own?'" Margie Anne asked.

At once, Raven began to pour out her heart with, "One-night, when I was supposed to be sleeping and Poppa was drinking with Everett Bass and Russell Russell, I heard Jude tell Maw that he was just plain lonely and had a-hankerin' to travel down towards New Orleans and work his way into becoming a big city merchant. And then he took her into the bedroom where I knew good and well he had no business being."

We listened.

"What could I do?"

Margie Anne shrugged.

Shrugging and twisting her long, curly black hair, "Anyhow, Poppa came home drunk as a skunk about dawn and caught them doing *you know what* in the bedroom. That's the last time I saw her and Jude because he took the shotgun to both of them. They flew straight out the front door, half naked, mind you, but they made it into Jude's wagon before Poppa could get a clear shot in. And took off!"

Margie Anne looked like she was going to faint from embarrassment before she took a deep breath and said, "Oh, Raven, you must have been brokenhearted at how foolish your Maw was to let a slick talker like that ruin her life and the ones she loved the most. Why I do declare, I bet you a dollar that she is sitting somewhere down in New Orleans this very minute crying her eyes out, missing you and your Poppa, and she's filled slam full of shame on account of the sin she committed against her own body that she let that City Slicker talk her into."

Raven's sapphire blue eyes lit up like two blue gems to the voice of Margie Ann's words before she asked, "You think so?"

"Why, sure! Time will tell. You wait and see," Margie Anne encouraged Raven.

She'll be offering to go with her down to New Orleans next.

Looking from us to the dusty wood, "Well, I doubt that, but I thank you for saying it anyhow," Raven said.

"Daddy says, 'Just trust in the Lord.' So, that's what I'd do if I were you. Yes, that's what I'd do," Margie Anne told her.

When I smiled at Raven, she turned to run.

"Wait! Johnny Paul Russell told us about you being a neighbor to Great Grandma Robinson along The Way. We are looking to get a glimpse of her and what lies behind the third waterfall. We want to learn some of the secrets of the People of The Way. Come back! *You hear?*" Margie Anne cried out.

"*Oh?* Johnny Paul Russell, I trust. His paw and my paw have been drinking together every weekend that passes since I can remember. Heck fire, Johnny Paul Russell and me are like family! Great Grandma Robinson is one of wise ones along The Way. I will take you to the third waterfall," Raven told us.

When I heard the word *family,* I sighed with the heavy feeling of loneliness. I began to wring my hands.

"Now, don't you be nervous or weary," she told me and turned to run away.

Margie Anne cried out, "Now, don't you go and run off!"

Raven stopped, looked back, and seemed to think a minute or two before she motioned for us to come and to follow her into the woods.

"What's she doing?" Margie Anne asked me.

"I think she wants us to follow her."

"Would you like a piece of Wrigley's Juicy Fruit?" Margie Anne asked me, reaching into her front pocket.

Reaching for the chewing gum, "Sure. Why don't you offer Raven a stick? Maybe that would help her to be less skittish," I replied.

"Hey, Raven, do you want some Wrigley's Juicy Fruit?" Margie Anne asked.

"Excuse me?" Raven replied.

Margie Anne was quick to say, "I said, do you want some chewing gum?"

In a flash, Raven was back with her hand stuck out. "Gosh—it sure is good to see somebody. I don't mean to run off like I do. I ain't seen nobody for about three days—other than the strays—and I get excited when I do. I don't know how to even act when a body comes near me, let alone *two!*" Raven told us; her bottom lip pleated. She set her sapphire blue eyes straight on me, "Can you two be trusted?"

I nodded.

Margie Anne said, "Oh, yes. I'm Margie Anne Roberts—the preacher's baby girl—and this is Myra Boone—the Reatha and Spurgeon Davis' newly found granddaughter from Merrihope—our neighbors."

She reached and tapped Margie Anne's shoulder and said, "My maw had thick glasses, too."

"She did?!" Margie shouted.

"Yeah. I remember she paid two dollars for them. I was with her at old Doc Farmer's office when she ordered them from Mobile, Alabama," she told Margie Anne.

"I got mine from Mobile, too," Margie Anne told her and held up her wristwatch for Raven to take a look at. They both smiled at each other while Raven admired the wristwatch.

"Would you two like to see what Will Falkner gave me to look after?" she asked.

"Sure!" we said in perfect unison.

"In case you don't know, Will Falkner is Judge Larry Falkner's boy. Judge Larry has a relative in Oxford named William Faulkner that's quite famous for writing. But he and Judge Larry ain't on the best of speaking terms. Will likes to think of himself as a writer, even though his Uncle William warned him that most folks don't give a hell about writers. Will has spent a great deal of time with his Uncle William up in Oxford. The old Faulkner man gave him many boxes filled with secret mystical, divine things that are beyond human understanding unless a body knows God. Even then, most folks can't see what they are used for unless they believe in the supernatural power of God. The boxes are packed slam full of what Will's Uncle William calls "Writer's Goods." And I look after the goods," she told us with pride in her voice.

"You can trust me—I used to write myself before the fire," I told her and started to cry.

Margie Ann spoke up and said, "Myra buried her folks a few months back. Her hands got burned in a fire in Merrihope. Sometimes when she looks at her scars, she starts with her crying spells. All she brought with her to Goodlife was herself. Why, even her clothes were given to her at the Opportunity House by the Children of Light."

Knowingly Raven said, "Let me see your hands."

I held out my hands for her to see.

"I heard along The Way that Enoch Vine prayed over some orphan with cripple hands once," she observed. "Are you that orphan?"

"I am," I said.

"I thought I recognized it to be you that Johnny Paul Russell and I saw from the woods."

I confirmed her recognition with a nod.

"Wait, can you believe no matter what you see or touch or hear and learn today?" Raven asked me.

"No, my faith is weak. And the more I think, the more I think my faith leaves me," I confessed.

"Along The Way, faith can be made perfect—that's the supernatural energy that draws us to God. Stop your crying so the blinders can fall from your eyes today. At The Way, you will not find your end but a beginning. Once we pass through the waterfalls, all your aggravations, shortcomings, and mistakes are no more. It's up to you, though. It's always up to you what to do once you know the truth and *how* to put it and *what* you learn to be truth to good use," Raven told me.

I nodded and took Margie Anne by the hand, who in the excitement of the moment, turned and gave me a kiss on the cheek.

And we were off.

The mystical Mississippi Piney Woods surrounded us with an avalanche of green kudzu vines assaulting dogwoods, magnolias, wisterias, and lilies fueled by more of the supernatural energy that seemingly drew us deeper into The Way.

A body can't help but feel protected in the Piney Woods.

Raven was carefree, floating in and out of the living and dying trees. I saw her turn into an ethereal spirit and begin to fly.

"How far are we from where you live?" Margie Anne asked her.

"I live in a hole in the ground along The Way. See, like I said before after Maw flew off with Jude Murphy, Poppa put me out one-night when he came home drunk. Poppa made me sit outside under a full moon the whole night long because he said that I looked just like her, especially with my long, curly black hair. See, I wouldn't let him cut my hair because Maw had always told me that the Bible says, 'a woman's long hair is her glory.'"

Margie Anne interrupted her. "And it does say that—it covers up her nakedness."

Making her way through more dying trees like the breath of an angel, "That's right. I wasn't about to cut my hair for nothing—unless Maw come back and give the word to do it. When Will Falkner saw a serpent wrapped around the moon that June night, he come looking for trouble and found me crying by what light was left in the sky. I told him my story, and he took me into The Way like one of his strays. I ain't seen Poppa since," she told us.

"Great day in the morning! I haven't heard of such a thing in all my born days—all night long, eh?" Margie Anne cried out.

From the air, Raven threw her head back and made a whistle-like bird call sound, and a mockingbird flew by and attempted to befriend her before flying back into a pine tree. When Margie Anne got a glimpse of the mockingbird, she stopped dead in her tracks, causing us to jerk back from our steady walking pace. Raven landed and gave Margie Anne a gentle smile that satisfied her before we were off again.

Stepping onto a narrow path, "It's right up here to the left," Raven said.

"How did you do *that?*" Margie Anne asked her.

"What?"

"How did you lift your body into the air like that and befriend a mockingbird?"

"Oh, I may not have too many *people* friends, but once I learned their ways, I've made lots of friends with the animals and all the creatures of the mystical Goodlife Piney Woods. See, I don't totally understand it myself other than that I was able to do more good once I made my choice to do 'good for evil' in the world."

"Do tell."

"Don't step on the speedwell," Raven told us.

I looked down and saw a bright blue cluster of flowers growing on top of the rocks.

Raven stopped and told us, "The Fall comes before we get to The Way. We can catch a glimpse of the People. Don't be afraid."

"We won't," we said in perfect unison.

Kicking away kudzu vines. "Close your eyes, relax, then release your faith and believe that you will be transformed from weak and mortal to strong and immortal, and then you can see what God wants you to see," she told us.

We obeyed. And when I opened my eyes, we were caught up in a celestial vision beyond human description amid a mystical green mist hovering over a tiny village swarming with people bent with age. I saw a Venus-like girl with salmon-pink skin carrying a Processional Cross studded with opaque stones and a linen cloth glowing with bright blue flowers. And there was a man clothed in lighted linen carrying a writer's inkhorn into a city that seemed to vanish in-and-out under the supernatural cloak of the green mist. Instead of a leader or a king sitting on a throne, I saw a headless lion sitting upon an altar that bore a walnut carving of the Massacre of the Innocents. A wild man wearing a vermillion fur-trimmed vest was riding a camel with tarnished silver reins, and birds and beasts flew around his head while he screamed unspeakable words.

"That's Veronica," Raven offered of the Venus-like girl carrying the Processional Cross.

Even though the old people were flesh and bone, as soon as their aged and bent bodies passed the headless lion, they instantly became young and straight again. I saw their years of sorrow, pain, and suffering melt away. In the blink of an eye, all were transformed into ethereal beings. They were flesh and bone no more.

"Where are they from?" Margie Anne asked.

Raven said, "All I know is they all crave what they don't have and that most come to The Way only to leave it again. Seldom do they stay and walk on its only street. They return to their own worlds like the rest of us."

"What is the name of the street?" I asked.

"Straight Street," she replied.

"Where's Great Grandma Robinson at?" I asked.

"If you don't see her before we enter the Fall's waters, then I suspect she's gone to Goshen," Raven said.

"We'll have to come back," I said.

"Is this where the Fountain of Youth is?" Margie Anne asked her.

"Nope. Amid the green mist, Veronica tells the People of the Way that the secret of life is death to self," Raven told us and kicked away at the kudzu vines. "Come—let's enter the Fall's waters."

We walked about fifteen yards until I saw a beautiful roaring waterfall. It was at least sixty-five feet high and had three hill-like layers that flowed over and down until the water trickled out into a stream, disappearing into the woods. We climbed a hill to get to its point of power.

"Let me see your scarred hands," Raven said to me.

When I hesitated, Margie Anne said, "You got to trust." So, I stuck out my hands, and Raven stuck them into the roaring waterfall letting the cold water flow over them until they became warm to the touch.

"Follow me," Raven told. "The Fall's waters can ease your pain but not take it away."

We three entered the Fall's crystal clear waters and crossed over to the other side, deeper into The Way. Once on the other side, we walked along a narrow road that was paved with sapphires. At the beginning of our walk, I saw the sun shining through trees adorned with all shapes and sizes of squirrels. The sky was an azure blue.

Holding onto her thick glasses and looking down, Margie Anne cried out, "Look at this pavement!"

Pointing in the direction of a pomegranate tree, "Be careful and watch for snakes! Up there, on the right, is a nest that we ain't been able to get shed of yet," Raven warned.

Margie Ann reached for a helping hand, and without reservation, forgetting about my own pain. I obliged her with one of mine. After many steps, we came upon an old cemetery with ancient marble and onyx headstones. Directly to its left was a bird sanctuary hidden by a cover of wire interwoven with limbs and vines, giving it a rounded dome of protection beneath the azure blue sky.

Margie Anne turned and asked me, "How do you feel?"

"The same."

"Remember what I said—that Veronica tells the People of The Way what the secret of life is?" Raven asked me.

"Yes, death to self. But what does that mean?" I asked.

Raven said, "Forget about your own pain and get your mind on others and how you can help them. Then your own pain will disappear. Faith is not seeing but believing in something with all your heart *even though* you cannot see it—yet."

"Do you mean that my scars may not ever disappear?" I asked.

"Well, I don't know about *that*, but I do know that Will Falkner told me that *battle scars* are what gets a body into the City of Heaven," she told me. "And from what I've seen of your hands, you've been battling for your own place there—that's for sure!"

When I saw two redwood picnic tables that looked plenty used, I asked, "Whose are those?"

Letting out a whistle, "That's where we all eat our meals together," she replied.

Suddenly, all sorts of stray animals came out from beyond The Way to move us forward on into our journey. There were kittens, puppies, chicks, squirrels, ducks, sheep, skunks, turkeys, two cows, a donkey, and a tiny black pig. In the distance, I saw some bunnies with a fat momma rabbit grazing alongside a pair of miniature horses.

"Would you look?" Margie Anne marveled and reached for a puppy. She brought it to her face and kissed it on the mouth before holding it to her heart. "Will sure loves strays, huh?"

"More than anything I'd say—except for writing," Raven said and reminded me of how much I missed Momma rocking and humming, "You Are My Sunshine," while she watched me copy words from the Bible all the daylong in Merrihope.

Eyeing the donkey, "I'd give anything for a pet," Margie Anne mused.

"His name is Mister Walter Hopkins," Raven offered.

When we nodded at Walter, he showed us his teeth and snorted.

"Can Mister Walter Hopkins talk?" Margie Anne asked.

"When he wants to talk, he can, but his hearing is weak. Walter, say something to my new friends!" Raven shouted.

Walter put his lips together and gave a short but sure whistle of "Down in My Heart."

Margie Anne lifted her eyebrows at the donkey who then gave us the cold shoulder and walked away.

"What about that sweet black pig?" I asked.

"Saint Anthony? Oh, he's mine. Stays and protects me every night that passes."

Looking all around for a house, "Where do you live?" I asked Raven.

"Up there on the right. Next to where Will has his place set up. Except I stay underground," she replied with a smile.

Shaking her head in amazement, "I haven't ever heard of anyone living underground before in all my born days," Margie Anne commented.

"Now you have. And, like I said, Will gave me an important job. At least he said that if his Uncle William had ever gotten the chance to meet me that he would have given me the exact same job on account of we both like horses," she said with pride.

When Margie Anne frowned at me, I gave her a shrug for a response.

We walked through a section of The Way that had cages full of hurt and maimed animals. Some were tied to fence-like posts while others were in colored cages of all sizes. Raven perked up and ran over to join them. And they all perked up as well and spoke in their own voices making animal sounds. There was a kitten in a box, a lamb in a cage, a dog tied to a post, a sparrow in a blue cage, and some rabbits in a pen off to the side of The Way.

"What now?" Margie Anne asked.

Reaching into a wooden box for a three-legged kitten, "These are all the throwaways—like me," Raven said, did little dance and whispered, "Hello, Stringer."

"Of all things—a three-legged kitten!" Margie Anne cried out.

With great gentleness, Raven placed Stringer into Margie Anne's hands and headed for another cage. She opened a latch, reached inside, and came back with a tiny lamb. Stroking its fluffy head, "This here's Zee—short for La-zina," she said.

Reaching for the lamb, "How about that? What's wrong with it?" I asked.

"It was born blind—no eyes whatsoever—not even sockets where they should have been. Nothing. Never seen such a blank face until I saw Zee's. Will said that he found her abandoned one-night while he was out catching June bugs in the moon glow," she told us.

Zee began to bleat.

Margie Anne put Stringer, the three-legged kitten, back into its box and just stood there like she was in another world with her eyes fixed on me until she came back to herself. She walked over to where I was standing and, holding the blind lamb, she reached into her front pocket and pulled out something wrapped in a brown napkin and bent her elbow up then inward to wipe a tear that had snuck out from behind her thick glasses. She unwrapped the brown napkin and out fell a biscuit, and a piece of meat, and a leaf of lettuce.

Offering the lamb, the lettuce and meat, "Here you go," she said before wrapping the biscuit back up and putting it back into her pocket. The lamb sniffed at the piece of meat, stuck out its tongue, and gave it a blind lick, nibbling only at the lettuce.

"Tear it up into little pieces or she won't eat it," Raven suggested before adding, "Will's about spoiled her rotten."

Margie Anne began to tear the lettuce into little pieces, and Zee took the lettuce—one piece at a time—while we all watched her in total silence, not saying so much as a single word as if we were all afraid that Zee would stop eating. And we certainly didn't want that to happen.

Walking towards an old shack, "This is Will Falkner's place," Raven said.

"Where is he?" I asked.

"Alone writing like always," she said. "Would you like to take a quick look inside?"

"Sure," I said.

Nodding, Margie Anne was quick to inquire, "Has he got any study books?"

"Shoot! Is study books all you ever think about?" I asked.

"Are. Just about," she replied with a smile.

Raven turned, and with a wistful look about her face, she asked me, "You miss your folks?"

"Very much," I told her.

"Me too," she said.

I shrugged, then chewed at my bottom lip.

"Know what I miss the most about mine?" she asked me.

"What?"

"I miss what we could have had as a family but never did. Ain't nothing in my life ever been normal or good either," she mused and led us up to the small wooden shack that had no door.

"I have a family—even a church family—and I feel the exact same way!" Margie Anne proclaimed. "Family members like church members can be as mean as rattlesnakes!"

Going into deep thought, *In the world as I've always known it; there is no such thing as a good life not even in Goodlife.* Coming back to myself, I asked, "Are we going inside that shack or not?"

"Yes. Let's just go on inside. I guess Will won't mind any. Besides, he keeps his Writer's Goods down in the ground where I stay."

The first thing I saw when we walked into the shack was an oval framed picture of an old, old man. Three chairs, an old couch, and three settees were positioned in a half circle. Someone had made a wall of that one-room shack into a bookcase of sorts. It wasn't beautiful or fancy, but somehow it possessed a defined strength of its own because of the way the books seemed to fit together. You couldn't have squeezed a mouse in if you had tried.

Margie Anne headed straight to study its contents before she sat down on the floor.

Tracing dust off the oval with her fingers, Raven told us, "That's Will's Great-Great-Grandfather Murray. He was a Scott, whatever *that* was," Raven told us.

Margie Anne announced from the floor, "A Scot is somebody from Scotland."

"Do tell," Raven said.

"Yes," Margie Anne confirmed.

"Will said that he was the *backbone* of the bunch because he was kind, gentle, and had strong principles. Every morning before breakfast was put on the kitchen table, it was understood that everybody that lived in his house would have a new Bible verse ready to recite at tongue-tip. And if you didn't have your Scripture ready, you didn't get one single bite of breakfast and not so much as a crust of bread. Will said there was an old maiden aunt who would help those who were short on words like his Uncle William *swot* up one verse in the front parlor. Will said his Great-Great-Grandfather Murray had sapphire blue eyes like mine, and once they were a-fixed on you, you knew you'd better have a new Bible verse ready to spit out or else," Raven informed us and held up a writing journal.

From the floor, Margie Anne laughed aloud to herself and the wall.

Raven asked me, "Where was your Paw from?"

"He moved from Florida to Mississippi. Why?"

"I think you are too pretty to be from the Union Community. You are *different*—in a good way."

"You are too."

"Really?"

"I think so."

"Maybe we are kindred spirits," Raven said with a smile and then led us out of the shack. "Come with me to my place. I'll show you what I believe I'm supposed to do with my life since I ain't ever going to be able to go to school like you two," she told us.

Smiling, Margie Anne said, "Last Friday was Myra's first day at Needles School."

Raven gave me a quizzical look when I shouted, "And I've decided to quit!"

"Why?" Raven asked me.

"The other children made fun of me! Called me mean names. Someone even stole my purse, emptied it, and then threw it behind a quince shrub. One boy, Cody Mack, even kicked my knee right out from under me when I was walking out of the classroom before two boys, Greg and Benny, picked me up and put me in a silver garbage can while the other children made fun of me and called me a retard, and a ba-boon girl! Oh, I hated school right off," I told her. "I don't aim to go back to Needles—or any school—ever!"

"I wouldn't care what names they called me—I'd go just to get out of here. Folks always called me and my people po' blacktop trash, anyway. Maybe I can go in your place?" Raven responded.

Margie Anne raised her eyebrows to me, but neither of us said another word.

After about twenty-five feet, Raven stopped near a mound of rocks next to a pomegranate tree. Kicking the dirt off what appeared to be a wooden door, "If it wasn't for Will, I don't know what I'd do or where I'd go. Why, he even brings me food from his house—The House of Joy and Life—and treats me like I'm just as good as the rest of his strays. His Maw, Lavender, sends me right fine coconut cake every third Sunday of the month. Johnny Paul Russell and I tend to find all sorts of interesting things people leave behind in the garbage dumps. I may eat scraps from the garbage, but I know in my heart I ain't po' blacktop trash! I have never had a body to help me outta the hole I'm in," Raven told us with earnest.

"My Lord, have mercy! Please don't call yourself a stray another time!" Margie Anne cried out.

"Anyhow, like I said before, Will said that his Uncle William would have wanted me to look after his Writer's Goods when he wasn't around. I'm just thankful somebody needs me for something if you want to know the truth about it. I'd trade places with you and take your scars to boot if I could have someone to love me once in a while. Hey, it wouldn't have to be every day that passed, but to hear the three words *I love you* once in a while, even if they didn't mean them, I wouldn't care. Hearing those three words would suit my fancy. Will told me that his Maw, Lavender, tells him that she loves him every day that passes. She even cooks hot food, and they all eat together and talk around a family table after his paw, Judge Larry, says grace. Will's Paw don't even drink whiskey like all the men-folks I know do. Why, I'd think I'd died and gone to the Promised Land if I had a family like that for one day of my life!" Raven cried out.

Margie Anne threw me a quizzical look.

"Stand back and I'll open the door into Mother Earth," Raven told us.

"What in the world?' Margie Anne asked.

"Oh, it's real nice down here and especially cool. I keep some sweet molasses around if you want something sweet to snack on, but other than that, all I got is water from the Fall."

"I am right thirsty. Aren't you, Myra?" Margie Anne asked me.

"Yes." I watched the great care that Raven used to open the wooden door.

"Good then! I can share a drink of water with *my* friends in *my* place," Raven said and sat down on the ground and motioned for us to do the same. And we did. She scooted sideways through the wooden door. We followed her every move before we took seven small steps deep down into Mother Earth.

Marveling while turning in little complete circles Margie Anne cried out, "Great day in the morning!"

There was a small but long bed covered with a finely twined linen bedspread made of a mixture of purple and blue and scarlet clothes with a yellow pillow in the shape of the sun at its head. The headboard was made of an old tree stump that looked to be as old as the world. On a small table, I saw a candlestick with three tree-like branches sticking out from both sides, and on the shelf were four cups made in the shape of almond blossom-like flowers—each having a calyx and petals on each side. A golden snuffer rested beside the candlestick next to a little tray filled with various types of eating utensils near two very gold snuff dishes.

I walked over to the corner of the room where I saw a shelf made of stone that was affixed to the wall. On the shelf was a golden cup, a silver spoon, an azure-blue lace handkerchief, a purple scarf, an embroidered sash made of finely twisted linen and blue, purple, and scarlet yarn. I saw a fine-twined piece of linen with little bits of gold and silver woven throughout, about two fistfuls of goat's hair, a stack of red-dyed ram's skins, and some goatskins, a stack of Atzei Shittim, acacia wood, and one vial of olive oil. There were various bottles of spices—pure myrrh, sweet cinnamon, and sweet calamus, cassia, and olive oil, and several cones of incense—stacte, onycha, galbanum, and pure frankincense, along with a box of tall kitchen matches. I saw two old crystal-clear lamps filled with olive oil that were sitting next to a bowl of water and a loaf of bread.

There was another chair in the corner near an oval mirror that was tacked into the dirt wall. One half of the wall was the original dirt while the other half had the same onyx and marble stones that I'd seen in the Soso cemetery. The onyx was worked into the marble, making various patterns like a black-and-white marble checkerboard. The floor was made of half dirt and half clear sapphire stones dusted with pine straw. A small stone crate sat on the floor and was packed with dull and smudgy cream-like writing materials with an old quill stuffed down in its side.

Pointing to the little stone crate, "What's this?" I asked.

"Parchment," Raven replied.

"What's it for?" I asked.

"Parchment?" Margie Anne asked the wall.

"Yes. Will says it's something he ain't quite figured out what to do with yet. I like the strip of azure blue virgin myself. It has a secret word written with the feather of a dove. His Uncle William told him to keep it dry, though, as well as those tools. The secret word will only be revealed to the Appointed One—in the Lord's time—when the birds hush their singing," she told us.

I saw that Will had a stack of old, worn-down books stacked one on top of the other. There were books by Dickens, Chekhov, Twain, Dostoevsky, Tolstoy, Shakespeare, Melville, Conrad, Cervantes, Anderson, Flaubert, Balzac, Simenon, Don Quixote, and Housman. I saw that there was a Bible sandwiched into another stack of what seemed to be poetry books by people like Wilbur, Marlowe, Champion, Jonson, Herrick, Donne, Keats, Eaton, and Shelley. I saw a book called "The Canterbury Tales" sitting on top of another titled "Paradise Lost."

I wonder if Will has read all these books.

I brushed the dust off a book titled "A Fable" with the tip of my finger and eyed a poem by Richard Wilbur that was tacked into the dirt wall that had "Southern Light" carved into the onyx.

"Where did you get all the pretty stones and things over on that stone shelf from?" I asked Raven, who was eyeing a picture postcard hanging near her head with *New Orleans* written in bright red lettering on it hanging near her head.

"This is all Will's doings. I don't know except what he tells me. He ain't ever told me how he come to find this place. I'm just happy to be here to look after the Mercy Seat," she beamed.

"*Mercy Seat?*" Margie Anne asked the wall.

"Uh, huh. Will said it's *my* place until I decide to leave Mother Earth," she said, walking closer to her bed as she went from squatting on her knees to lying flat on her stomach to sprawling out on the floor while feeling under the bed.

"What in the Sam Hill are you doing?" I asked.

Raven ignored me.

Margie Anne moved in to get a closer look.

I bent forward to see what she was searching under the bed for.

"Is she having a *fit* like some of them mentally retarded folks do over at the Ellisville State School when no one shows up to take them home on a holiday?" Margie Anne whispered to me.

"How would I know?" I said, knowing that she and Brother Jim Roberts took as many as would fit into the Soso church bus to their house each and every holiday that passed for dinner with a real bona fide family even if her Maw never got out of the bed and showed her face to the lot of them.

Margie Anne laughed to herself, got down on the floor, and joined Raven. "This is the prettiest floor—even if it is half dirt, isn't it?" she asked her.

Raven did not reply. Instead, she began to pull on a thick rope and gave Margie Anne a nod as if to signal for help. Margie Anne obliged her, and they both began pulling while I watched until Raven cried out, "Myra, don't just stand there watching! Help us!"

I hit the dirt along with them.

"Lord, it sure is heavy," Margie Anne remarked.

Raven looked at the floor and said, "I'm stronger than I look. I've moved it by myself before. Will must have pushed it back too far the last time he got it out."

Without warning, something strange shot out from under the bed. It was a box that looked as old as Time. The outside was overlaid in pure gold with an even more gold molding draped higher around its top. Each corner held a golden ring where seemingly two golden poles could fit through for easy carrying. The lid of the box was made of one solid piece of gold with glowing cherubim sitting at each end — each one facing the other — both looking down at the lid. Their wings rested inside a hole within the old box.

Stroking and marveling at the top of one of the cherub's heads, Margie Anne cried out, "In all my born days — I never thought I'd see... Of all things — the pure Art — I mean Ark!"

I heard a cherub stir. I realized that in our presence, the cherub's wings had begun to flutter and fill the air with their timeless gold of old.

Raven stood up and smiled.

Eyeing the gold box, Margie Anne exclaimed, "Oh, my goodness! Why, it looks like the work of a pure artist, doesn't it?"

"What Ark?" I asked.

"Moses' Ark — not the boat Ark that Noah made, but *The Ark of the Testimony* that God ordered made to hold the Ten Commandments.

Yes, it is indeed the lost Mercy Seat! I recognize it from what the Bible tells us about it," Margie Anne said with total Roberts' excitement.

Raven beamed, and her sapphire eyes were glowing.

Margie Anne cried out, "Written by the pure finger of God! Yes, straight on top of old Mount Sinai pretty near where the Red Sea is where it all happened. It took right at forty or so days to finish up the Ten Commandments."

"I don't know nobody named Moses, but I do know that Will's Uncle William told him this: 'The secret spiritual and mystical things belong to the Lord our God, but sometimes those secret things are revealed to the children so that we may do all the works of the law.' And this here old box is one of them *secret spiritual and mystical things* that went along with his Writer's Goods," Raven told us.

"Boy, my daddy would sure like to look at this here Ark—that's for sure. Do you think that he could come and visit you?" Margie Anne asked Raven, who was shaking her head a sure and steady no.

"No! Will's going to have a fit anyhow when or if he finds out you two were here. I ain't even sure why I trusted you myself. I suppose I was just so alone and needed somebody to talk to. It ain't easy not having anybody but yourself and a bunch of strays and all this junk to keep dusted. Anyway, no one can see it—not before the appointed time. And only Will or his Uncle William can make that decision—even if he must make it from the grave one day," she replied, getting up and heading for a pitcher of water. She poured the water into three golden cups, placed them on a tarnished silver tray, and walked over and offered us a drink.

"Aren't you going to open it up for us to see?" Margie Anne asked.

"It has never been opened—not that we know of, that is. But if you like, we can try to rattle it and listen to the stones inside shake," she said, offering us a drink of water while she softly sang, *Scuttles and cans, buttons and bows. I'll cure your ills, and I'll cheer your woes.*

The cherubim's wings continued to flutter and dust the floor with their timeless gold of old amid a green mist that was slowly surrounding us.

Margie Anne reached into her front pocket and brought back the brown napkin and unwrapped the biscuit she had saved. She began to break the bread into three equal pieces. She offered Raven one. I took a piece, and she took the last piece and sat down on the floor. Raven lay down beside her and put her head on top of the Mercy Seat and gave us a sad look. She took a deep breath and began twisting her long, curly black hair before she bent down and kissed one of the cherubim on the head. She smiled at Margie Anne, who reached over and gave her a hug filled with nothing but pure love.

I broke into a cold sweat wondering how in the world I would make it without my folks. I felt alone and helpless until like two adopted sisters Margie Anne Roberts and Raven raised their golden cups to me and smiled. We continued to drink water and share in little bites of bread like three hungry sparrows nesting on a floor made of dirt, pine straw, and sapphire stone that the cherubim had slowly dusted with the timeless gold of God's *once lost now found* Mercy Seat.

After a while we stood to our feet. Then we three dropped to our knees—not to pray but to write the hidden secrets of our hearts with our Jupiter fingers in the gold dusted floor in a hole deep within Mother Earth somewhere along The Way. As I watched the green mist continue to fill the air around us, I made the silent choice to go to school every year from then on out so that I could learn how to help myself and children like Raven, Margie Anne Roberts, Johnny Paul Russell, and even those I didn't know but would come to know—amid and far beyond—my neighbors.

A study guide that suggests a plausible, actionable way to reach the institutional and library market AND foreign markets in both English and translation. A Human Geography course can be crafted around "My Neighbors, Goodlife, Mississippi" and "Goodlife, Mississippi" to teach students about the source of place—names and local dialects and the anthropology of place—in other words, *What Made Mississippi: Mississippi*.

Myra Boone and the Varieties of Spiritual Experiences in My Neighbors, Goodlife, Mississippi and Goodlife, Mississippi

"My Neighbors, Goodlife, Mississippi" (Eileen Saint Lauren, ©2022) and "Goodlife, Mississippi" (Eileen Saint Lauren, ©2022) a novel based on the emergence of authentic faith in its heroine, Mary "Myra" Boone, offers a rich, intellectually bracing platform to help students understand—in a direct, visceral way—three masterworks of theology which appear in the liberal arts catalogues of major colleges and universities:

• **William James –***The Varieties of Religious Experiences: A Study in Human Nature* (1902)
• **Rudolph Otto –***The Idea of the Holy* (1917)

- **Mircea Eliade** *–The Sacred & the Profane* (1957)

In this light, "My Neighbors, Goodlife, Mississippi" and "Goodlife, Mississippi" delivers a framework for course-length introductions to modern theology. In pairing readings by James, Eliade and Otto with the text of Saint Lauren's richly textured fiction, students will learn and apply the opposing skills of *exegesis* and *eisegesis* to their reading of Saint Lauren's novel and these theological classics. For students enrolled in Spiritual Studies or seminary curricula, these paired readings will strengthen the objective, interpretive skills students apply to their readings of Scripture.

Theme: Quest, Struggle and Celebration

In vernacular language reminiscent of Flannery O'Connor, William Faulkner, and Charles Spurgeon, "My Neighbors, Goodlife, Mississippi" and "Goodlife, Mississippi" explores the elements of quest, struggle, and celebration the child encounters in a quest for meaning—or what Eliade terms the "sacred"—as she moves through a secular life both "profane" and grotesque. In other words, she must experience ungodly events and survive outrageous events to grasp the significance of her fellow-characters, from the five orphaned girls she meets in "The Opportunity House" (who represent certain Saints and Disciples) to Paula (who is the confident, reassuring embodiment of Saint Paul) to their overseer, Moloch, the Devil incarnate (John Milton and William Shakespeare).

Structure: Sacred Space, Time, Nature, and Self

An introductory theology course based on Saint Lauren's fantastic magical realism will focus on the rudiments of spiritual study this writer evokes with depth and intensity. They are: sacred space, time, nature and self.

Sacred Space

In sacred spaces such as the City of Goodlife or Enoch's Glass House in, "My Neighbors, Goodlife, Mississippi," Myra experiences a taste, then a full serving, of Heaven. As she passes through the fire of her family's burning house, she glimpses first purgatory then hell, yet emerges with new life. In a more profound way, and guided by Eliade's evocative account of biblical time, Myra's journey represents the concept of the *eternal return*, the endless process by which the seeker abandons with childlike innocence her path to the sacred, but still returns to the road and reaches her holy destination. It represents, perhaps, a path to the physical church.

Sacred Time

It is at this point, Otto's concept of the Holy, the *Mysterium Tremendum*, the awe, relief, and revelation the seeker feels as she arrives Home—intervenes. As Otto writes: "[this] gentle tide pervades the mind with the deep tranquility of worship." At this juncture, the instructor might ask: Is the seeker's arrival in Heaven temporary or permanent? Is she doomed to repeat the sequence—as some Eastern faiths suggest—or has she actually *returned*? Christianity espouses the return without repetition. It is one reason why the faith relies deeply—as Myra does—on locales (such as Goodlife—a symbol of the new Jerusalem) on physical space (such as the Union Community Church—symbolic of the Duke Chapel and / or the Canterbury Cathedral) and on objects the piece of Cross wood and the Ark of the Covenant—"My Neighbors, Goodlife, Mississippi"—(ranging from relics of the True Cross to rosaries and medallions.)

It is noteworthy that Myra's picaresque journey is non-linear. Her travels are described without a predictable chronology. This suggests that the seeker's quest—though the lens of consciousness—relies on an internal, spiritual clock. By focusing at intervals on *sacred time*, Myra lives within the Near Eastern, even Judaic, realm of the Sacred.

Myra is a wanderer, or nomad, just as the People of the Pentateuch were. Their *40 years* had supernatural significance and their *Sabbath* became the fulcrum of survival. In their harsh and transient world, there were few structures beyond the pyramids in which travelers could find shelter. Indeed, the Ark of the Covenant seems dwarfed by the vast space over which it travelled just as it is in the setting of "My Neighbors, Goodlife, Mississippi" and "Goodlife, Mississippi" and found in both books.

In Myra's life, we also experience the significance of Eliade's temporal concepts of *cosmos and chaos*, so crucial to an understanding of Genesis 1 and 2, and to the repeated ways in which the Old Testament God generated order from chaos. In the spirit of Genesis,

Myra, the seeker is also a creator. She surmounts and transforms her disabilities into strength, obstacles into pathways, doubts into faith.

Sacred Nature

Saint Lauren's text explodes with natural imagery. There are symbolic breezes stirring the treetops, inner tempest storms that rock the reader's foundations, bursts of fire in Merrihope, family members that give up the Ghost into the starlit sky, and sun-rings encircle a character's head in Goodlife. Characters anoint one another with olive oil, and whales and prophets on stain glassed windows. Flies speak words of darkness, and the Piney Woods offer holy solace and shelter. The sun rises and the moon sets at conspicuous times. Water exercises its magic and the great sky—azure dome or pitch black—is ever-present.

In this way, "My Neighbors, Goodlife, Mississippi" and "Goodlife, Mississippi" invokes the *hierophany* (holy, sacred) of nature as Eliade defines it, a universe packed with myriad signs and symbols. In the Saint Lauren's work, natural phenomena are characters which appall, invite, warn, destroy, and shelter both seekers and spiritual predators.

In the author's vivid descriptions of natural phenomena, from emesis to rain, she envisions a world of volcanic meaning. In James' model of spiritual experience, worship cannot occur without sensory experience, whether one finds holiness in the incense of a processional or the solitude and fragrance of wild places. Using exegetical skills, students will learn to discern the holy as Myra does, where she does, *as she does.*

Sacred Self

Myra's deformed body is eventually transformed. Myra seems always to be the *unformed* child on the edge of adolescence, a period in of *initiation* in both James and Eliade's work.

In this light, John Durham, notes in notes on Eliade's *The Sacred & Profane 4* at <Bytrentsacred.co.uk> "…Initiation rites imparted three kinds of *revelation*: about the sacred, about death and about sexuality. They [subjected] initiates to symbolic death followed by rebirth as a new person."

The Sacred Self is Myra's destination. While her arrival may seem anti-climactic to some readers, Saint Lauren depicts the emergence of the Sacred Self as a life-long process. In order to achieve rebirth, death in all its forms is a prerequisite, and Myra approaches spiritual death at intervals throughout this sequence of picaresque story telling.

Myra Boone and the Varieties and Spiritual Experience in My Neighbors, Goodlife, Mississippi, and *Goodlife, Mississippi*

In Jamesian terms, Myra Boone is a "spiritual genius" armed by Eliade's Creator to conquer any dragons which block her from recognition, or revelation, of the "Holy." In Jamesian terms, Myra has "mystical consciousness" and indeed, Saint Lauren's narrative voice is instilled in Myra's, a character who succumbs to spiritual trances and awakens to mystical, transcendent experience repeatedly.

Again, in Jamesian terms, Myra's stories take the divided self with which she begins her tale and reconciles the dichotomy through rebirth and revelation. Had James read Saint Lauren's manuscript, his final question would be whether Myra's rebirth—or second awakening—was enough. Should we expect yet another rebirth?

It is fitting, then, in tribute to Saint Lauren's work and James' deeply pragmatic nature that we quote James' general philosophical position on God's existence as follows:

"I have no hypotheses to offer beyond what the phenomenon of 'prayerful communion'... suggests ...The only thing that it unequivocally testifies to is that we can experience union with *something* larger than ourselves and that, in that union, we find our greatest peace."

The synonym of grace to "peace" can be applied to maintain this deeply emotional work to help illuminate the rudiments of active spirituality.

FORTHCOMING BY THE AUTHOR

BATTLE FOR LOVE

Printed in the USA
CPSIA information can be obtained
at www.ICGtesting.com
LVHW011520141223
765934LV00009B/1